Mr. Gunderson's
Home Economics

Facing the Father Factor

RODNEY E. WALKER

WESTBOW·
PRESS
A DIVISION OF THOMAS NELSON
& ZONDERVAN

Biblical references were taken from the New King James Version. Copyright © 1979, 1980, 1982 by Thomas Nelson, inc. Used by permission. All rights reserved.

WestBow Press books may be ordered through booksellers or by contacting:

WestBow Press
A Division of Thomas Nelson & Zondervan
1663 Liberty Drive
Bloomington, IN 47403
www.westbowpress.com
1 (866) 928-1240

ISBN: 978-1-4908-3987-5 (sc)
ISBN: 978-1-4908-3988-2 (hc)
ISBN: 978-1-4908-3989-9 (e)

Library of Congress Control Number: 2014910264

Printed in the United States of America.

WestBow Press rev. date: 06/19/2014

If Young Girls ~A

If Human Trafficking ~B

If Broken Homes ~C

<u>If Fathers ~D</u>

Then A ÷ C − D = B P(Human Trafficking)

Rodney E. Walker

CONTENTS

CHAPTER 1

Every year, the unidentified bodies of about five thousand adolescents are buried in unmarked graves throughout the nation. Their families will never discover where or how they died. Some are runaways. Some were victims of kidnapping or human trafficking. What most have in common is that they are high school dropouts under the age of eighteen from unstable families—troubled kids who lost confidence in public education and in themselves.

It was a morning like any other when Theresa Jezebel Jablanski, an eleventh grader, overslept, leading her to miss her first class. She didn't care. She woke up after another night of sleeping with her nose ring still in to save herself time in the bathroom before leaving the house. Sometimes, her add-on fingernails made it difficult to find the puncture opening in her nose cartilage, which often consumed considerable time.

She descended the stairs and shuffled her 113-pound body into the kitchen, where she found her mother's usual message on a sticky pad.

Waffles in freezer. Unplug the toaster when you're done.
If I'm not back by 6:30, pop in a TV dinner. You have
my cell number.

Love ya,
Mom

Theresa wanted to hurt herself but didn't understand why. Many of her peers admired her. She was blonde and intelligent, and her catlike features suggested a career in acting or television journalism, but she was hurting. As usual, she decided against warming up a plate of waffles and ate an apple instead. She knew that there was something about the chemistry in apples that reduced hunger pangs. She rarely ate lunch.

Apple core in hand, she ran back upstairs to retrieve her cell phone from underneath her bed covers. Since she sometimes woke up in the middle of the night and checked her text messages, she slept with her phone. She grabbed her book bag, slipped on her pumps, and walked outside to her mint-green Ford Taurus.

Theresa arrived at Sandpebble High School two hours late. Then she slipped away an hour early, missing her last class.

Ms. Jablanski's daughter was making trouble at home, and Ms. Jablanski could no longer hide that fact behind the apparent success of her career. She headed the human resources department at a large construction firm and was well educated and always well dressed; every skirt directed attention to the blood-red rose tattoo on her left ankle. Despite several failed romantic relationships with employees at the office, many people liked Ms. Jablanski, but everyone suspected that she was not raising her daughter properly, and now she was attending her second Parent-Teacher Association conference meeting to seek help and vent her feelings.

Ms. Jablanski was angry.

"All I know is that somebody has to do something," she said. "Theresa might have had her moments before, but now she's skipping classes, and she can't afford to be held back. It's those friends she hangs around with—those bad kids. She's changing the way she dresses, she's always on the phone now, and I just about died when I saw that nose ring! Why does the school allow the kids to pierce themselves like that?"

"We aren't the parents," said Mr. Meeks, an administrator. "We can't tell them what type of friends to have or prevent them from piercing their noses. Theresa bought that nose ring just next door to the tattoo studio where you had your own tattoo done, Ms. Jablanski."

"If you don't mind my asking," he continued with mounting tension, "don't you think that your own lifestyle might be sending mixed messages to your daughter? I'm just trying to be real with you."

Ms. Jablanski jerked back in her seat, the pink leather purse she'd held on her lap crashing to the floor. "How dare you!" she yelled. "How dare you suggest that I'm negligent! I love my daughter and would do anything for her. Everyone knows that!"

"No one is saying that you're negligent, honey," one of the parents said, her voice soothing. "What I think Mr. Meeks is saying is that our kids' value systems are formed at home. We're the primary role models, no matter how many friends they have or how much junk television they watch. I had to learn that the hard way when my husband returned from a six-month tour in the Middle East last year."

"I apologize if I've offended you," said Mr. Meeks, setting down a cup of black coffee, "but this is your second PTA meeting, and all I've ever heard from you is that you want the school district to fix something that can only be dealt with at home. Please, evaluate your own relationship with your daughter. We understand that her father is not in her life now, but don't you think she ought to be able to see him?"

"No, I don't," Ms. Jablanski responded, wiping away the traces of black mascara that smudged her flushed face.

Meeks looked at the seven mothers attending the meeting and said, "Ladies, I'm going to tell you something that one of our psych counselors told me yesterday. She said that, after ten years as a counselor, she's actually considering a career change now because the parents just aren't getting it. They're not investing in the relationships they have with their kids. They may say they love their kids, but she says that more than half of the parents she talks to don't know how to love in practical ways. They just want to be their children's friends, so they give them all the latest gadgets and computer games, which only spoils them.

"And the girls—this is a growing concern. I know the local TV stations have done a good job covering our girls' scholarship awards and soccer games, but they're not touching stories about the increase in teen pregnancy and prostitution in our community. They won't say anything about the rate of homelessness that is skyrocketing for high-school-aged single mothers in this county or the growing rate of mental illness. We have ten girls who have been diagnosed with clinical depression in the local school district. The counselor told me that fixing the problem would mean visiting the homes and talking about how people are living. That's what it's come to." At this point every mother, except Ms. Jablanski, was leaning forward in their seat.

"It was this counselor's opinion that half of the problems with our girls would begin to disappear if they just spent more quality time with their fathers. She's amazed at how ignorant many mothers these days are about the development of healthy young women. They need to have their femininity reaffirmed by a masculine source. They need to know they're lovable, beautiful, and wanted by a man."

Mr. Meeks turned to Ms. Jablanski, adding, "That's why, Ms. Jablanski, they become vulnerable to running around in the wrong crowd of boys. I'm talking about these saggy-pants, convict-cultured losers who'll take advantage of your daughters and bring them to ruin. It's happening right here—right before our eyes. You can go down to the local post office and see the faces of twelve missing teenage girls who were registered at schools in our local district last year."

This exchange was typical of the new tone of discussions at the Sandpebble High Charter School PTA meetings, which more often than not featured heated discussions about the personal frustrations of administrators, open rebukes, and admitted failures among the parents. They had all initially bought into the school's vision of promoting academic excellence and holistically shaping the character of the student body to turn out well-adjusted, intelligent, healthy young men and women. However, that vision was fading as the sobering realities of deviant and self-destructive behavior among the youth became the center of attention and shame.

The Sandpebble High Charter School was still fairly new. Since the local public school district approved it as a start-up charter school, it was seen as their crowning achievement. However, now the rising tide of troubled adolescents made many administrators feel old. The principal and even members of the local city council had worked hard to suppress news reports about three recent teen suicides and felt fortunate that the local news directors understood how such stories could negatively affect tourism and small businesses in the area. Nonetheless, the school was losing patience with its undesirables, its intellectually handicapped gangsters, its unwed and unashamed teen mothers, its underachieving marijuana addicts and bullies in the student body.

The Board of Directors scrambled to make a change. They called for the implementation of several alternative classroom-management programs designed to educate new teachers in more therapeutic methods of handling middle and high school students. There was the democratic model, in which every student had an equal vote concerning classroom issues, but outvoted students had begun to take sides, one against another, and the divisions resulted in escalating violence on the school grounds and school buses. Teachers then tried a meritocracy model, in which students were rewarded for their achievements with money. The effort, funded through a "petty cash" fund appropriated through the school budgets, worked well for two months, before the overachieving, "smart" students began to be jumped, robbed, and threatened by their jealous classmates. The new programs lasted no longer than the new teachers did.

Although the district had started the school in response to an unprecedented interest in "holistic education," some parents were now thinking about withdrawing their children. The school's facilities were in the avant-garde of modern public architecture, and the local parents were profiled as middle- to upper-middle class, but the students were overwhelmingly from single-parent homes, and too many stressed-out parents were simply out of touch with their children. A small number of troublemakers began to create problems on the campus, which was seeing an increase in illegal drug paraphernalia, and increasing numbers of adolescent girls joined the fad of texting seminude images of themselves to first-string football players. Administrators were desperate to stop the rising tide of inappropriate behavior.

CHAPTER 2

The teachers' lounge was abuzz with crosstalk about the latest classroom drama. Ms. Henderson, who taught social studies, was recounting an incident that had occurred during her first period.

"Then I told him I didn't care how much his mother spent on that iPad; he would either have to put it away or I would confiscate it and take it to the principal's office. So do you want to know what he did? He told me to smile and snapped a picture of me with that thing while I was still talking to him. Then he threatened to post it on the Internet tonight."

"You should've called security the first minute he refused to put it away," said Mr. Tate, who taught American history. "I would've taken it from him, snapped a photo of his mug and told him I was going to the local police precinct to show the photo. That kid's gotta be wanted for something. I'll bet if they run a check on his driver's license he'll show up wanted for unpaid traffic tickets or something."

"Well, when security finally got there," continued Ms. Henderson, "he decided to put it away—but that doesn't change the fact that he snapped my picture right in class. Anyway, he's supposed to stay after school to talk with the principal, and you can bet I'll get there early."

The Social Studies department chair walked into the lounge wearing a sober expression, which was unusual because he was usually lighthearted and easygoing; even the junior and senior girls admired him for his charismatic personality. All eyes were upon him now as the lounge crosstalk came to a halt.

"What's up, David?" said Mr. Tate. "You don't look happy." David's left hand was fidgeting with keys in his pocket.

"Just got back from the weekly admin meeting," said David. "We're going to have a department meeting after school." The others in the room groaned, and David smiled. "Don't worry, it won't be too long. Just make sure you sign the sign-in sheet in room 301."

"What is it?" another teacher asked. "Are they cutting staff in our department?"

"No, but there are some changes being proposed that could affect us. I wouldn't worry about anything. Just be there at three."

Three o'clock seemed an eternity away. The day dragged on, from student announcements on the PA system, to a monthly fire drill, to five underclass male students' being escorted out of the school, to the principal's announcing a canned-soup drive over the PA. Finally, the students were dismissed.

Since there were still a dozen doughnuts on the verge of expiration left in the lounge refrigerator, a few of the teachers in David's department gathered them up, along with twelve paper plates, a stack of napkins, and a half liter of apple juice. When they got to room 301, however, the whole department was already there, waiting.

David walked into the room with a clipboard and a yellow notepad in his hands. Department meetings had a tendency to trigger strong emotions. "I'm glad to see that everyone made it to this one," he said, picking up the sign-in sheet, "but what happened to Ms. Henderson?"

"She had to run down to the principal's office for a meeting about one of her students," said Mrs. Dixon, "you know, that kid with those ugly tattoos up his neck? Well, he's got an iPad now, and he took a picture of her—"

"Oh, yes, that's right," David said. "I was told about that. Well, if she doesn't make it here, could someone fill her in on this meeting? She needs to hear this." One of the teachers nodded.

David walked to the corner of the room, stood behind the podium, and rested his notes from the administration meeting on it. Then he began, "I know that nobody here has forgotten our last meeting, when I announced how the school wants us to deal with child obesity, and I'm glad to say that nothing was mentioned about that program at the admin meeting today. I know it's been a burden for some of you to keep up your data on student profiles with their body mass indexes and all the paperwork that goes into that, but if we don't do it, it could result in a loss of funds. I want you to remember that one of the things that's supposed to make us different as a charter school is that we're holistic. We're supposed somehow to make these kids better in body, mind, and spirit, in addition to academic excellence. I know they told you this at the orientation."

"Hey, Dave," interrupted a history teacher, "I think we all know that our fat kids are not gonna get any thinner just because the kitchen people are mixing more soy beans in their hamburger. But if it keeps the grant money coming in, you'll have no complaints from me."

"I'm just happy they haven't asked us to follow up on these kids to record any weight loss," said Mrs. Mahoney from medieval history. "Could you imagine if the Board ever asked for proof to see if this program is working? We'd never see the end of the paperwork."

"You know, they may just do that sometime, but I think they'd hire more staff in the nursing department for that kind of thing," said Mrs.

Dixon from social studies. "I'm sorry, but the obese kids aren't going to get much better until things start changing at home. We really can't do anything about it here. I blame those young mothers. These kids are living on fast food morning day and night. Their mothers aren't cooking decent meals anymore because their priorities are all screwed up!"

"I wouldn't put all the blame on them," protested Ms. Wilkerson from psychology. "They probably have so much more to do now."

"Baloney!" Mrs. Dixon said with a dismissive wave of hand. "I'll bet I'm as busy as they are, working full time, and I'm still able to make it home before Bob and the kids get there and have a balanced dinner prepared. That's why good men don't stay with them—I'll have to tell you about my niece sometime."

"Whoa, now," chuckled Dave. "Let's not make this like our last meeting, okay? There's too much on our plate now, and I'm sure most of you want to beat the traffic going home. I need to tell you that something's coming up about what they're now calling our kids' emotional intelligence." Several of the teachers began to speak, but David raised a hand to stop them. "Now, before you start asking questions, I know what you're thinking: If you're like me, emotions and intelligence don't mix too well, and I still don't buy into this harebrained theory, but this is how things are going to go now. They're looking for ways that we can assess the emotional intelligence of students."

Before David could stop him, Mr. Tate interrupted. "Are you gonna tell us now that we gotta counsel these kids? When are we ever going to get back to teaching?"

David shook his head. "Nobody's going to have to counsel anyone, and they're not targeting the whole student body—just the troublemakers. Everybody pretty much knows who they are."

"Okay, okay, wait a minute," said Mr. Tate. "So we're gonna have to spend time interviewing our troublemakers, assuming that they're going to cooperate, and assess their so-called emotional intelligence? I think it's the people behind this program who don't have any emotional intelligence! It's junk science!"

The teachers continued in their grumbling, and David had to raise his voice to be heard over them. "Listen," he said, his voice growing tense, "I haven't even told you how it works!" The teachers quieted down and David lowered his voice again. "They've got a computer template for us, and all we have to do is fill in little bubbles during class—you can do it during roll call. If the kid looks depressed or drugged out, just click on a bubble on your desktop. It'll be sent in with attendance, and the admin staff will sort it all out and compile reports for the counseling staff."

"Dave," asked Mrs. Dixon, "does this affect our grant funding?"

"You bet it does."

"But what do they plan to do with the results? All they'll have is a stack of reports on confused kids with bad attitudes."

"Good question—and this is where we all come in. They're adding a new home economics course to our department to help the troublemakers graduate. Some of the slower or problem kids will be able to choose it as an elective to fulfill their math or social studies requirements for graduation."

The teachers were silent until Ms. Henderson asked, "Who is supposed to teach this new course? They phased home ec. out fifteen years ago."

"The district has decided that all of us in this department have the right credentials to teach the course, but I suggested that they hire a new home ec. teacher and that any of us could be stand-in substitutes if need be."

In unison the teachers sighed in relief. No one thought they could survive two weeks in a class full of their troublemakers, and no one would have been willing to try.

"There is one catch to this new program," Dave continued, his eyes on his notes. "Part of it is being funded by the local Catholic diocese, which means it can be taught from a Judeo-Christian worldview. What they're saying is that there ought to be a moral base to this course to teach about right and wrong choices."

"I don't remember home ec. addressing any moral issues when I had to take it thirty years ago," said Mrs. Dixon.

"I thought the same thing," said Dave, "but when you think about it, home ec. used to cover issues about roles within the family, family relationships, differences between men and women, and setting family budgets."

"Family?" exclaimed Mr. Tate. "Listen, they've redefined the family so much that I'd be embarrassed to talk about family today."

"This course is going to be different. Remember, it's to be taught from a Judeo-Christian worldview. I'm sure that only the traditional family model will be taught."

"I might want to teach this course myself," said Mrs. Dixon.

CHAPTER 3

Keith W. Gunderson was still in his bathrobe as he sat at the breakfast table with his Bible in hand. His wife, Janet, had to drop the children off at school early that morning because she had volunteered to chaperone her daughter's class on a local field trip. Since the field trip bus had to leave fifteen minutes before school started, the Gunderson family had only a brief time for family prayer before breakfast that day.

Gunderson was an African American retired air force chaplain who was reentering the job market. His family had lived seven years in Europe and was now a bit out of touch with the latest cultural trends in the United States. However, it wasn't their prolonged absence that made their cultural surroundings seem so alien; it was their faith.

After meditating about biblical verses for half an hour, Gunderson thanked God for the day that lay before him and picked up the morning newspaper. He opened it to an editorial. "Without a doubt," it read,

> yesterday's sex scandal at the St. Longinus all boys' school is a disgrace to our community. The boys who took those digital photos of the girls at the Sandpebble Charter High School should all have their faces posted

on Facebook as youth predators, and then their parents should be sued.

But this event is more than a disgrace, as it prompts a question: How is it that a group of young men at one of the most prestigious schools in our county can act like this? There has never been any record of such behavior in their past, and some of them are honor students. Many of them will go on to prestigious universities and become doctors and lawyers. How could they engage in this type of behavior? St. Longinus teaches high moral principles, and the boys have track records of being exemplary on campus. But what happens when they leave their campus? How will these boys ever know how to treat women, when they start doing things like this at such a young age? Why do so many young men degrade the image of our young women?

Gunderson closed the newspaper and sighed. Then he thought. And then it was there: an impetus to respond. Gunderson knew that he was being led to respond to the editorial, but he also knew that what he wanted to write would be controversial. However, in faith, he decided to put his thoughts to paper.

"Dear Editor," he wrote,

I agree wholeheartedly with you concerning the questions you raised pertaining to the integrity of the boys at St. Longinus. Indeed, sneaking obscene photos of young girls and posting them on online social networks is unacceptable behavior that must be addressed. However, there is also a larger issue: As the father of daughters I have addressed these issues with my girls, but I feel that I'm in a shrinking minority. You raised some good questions about the boys at St.

Longinus, but these boys may have been responding to something they saw in these girls.

My family and I have lived overseas for about seven years. When we came back Stateside, we were shocked to see how base the youth culture had become, and we're still adjusting to it. To be frank, in most parts of the world, girls who dress like many of our daughters dress in high school are seen as prostitutes, and many of them are in fact. We like to harangue dirty old men who watch pornography—I'm not defending pornography at all, don't misunderstand me—but pornography is a billion-dollar industry in this country that is fueled by the willful acts of our women. Thousands of young women, older women, and businesswomen—mothers too—are shamelessly doing these things, yet we dare to wonder why the young men are losing respect for young women? There is a "girls gone wild" culture all around us, and no one is holding these young women accountable for respecting themselves. Instead, we want to make them heroes and talk about their achievements as we push them to try to outdo the boys. Let's open our eyes: Some of the girls at the Sandpebble Charter school had posted seminude photos of themselves online before those immature St. Longinus boys sought them out.

I will end this letter with a question in response to your question. You asked why so many young men disrespect young women. I ask why so many young women disrespect themselves.

K Gunderson, loving father and husband.

Gunderdson slipped the letter into an envelope, addressed it to the editor of the newspaper, and went back to reading his paper, where he noticed an ad in the classified section for a home ec. teacher at Sandpebble Charter High School. It called for a credentialed teacher who was willing to teach a new course from an ethical Judeo-Christian worldview. The ad was only a day old. Immediately, Gunderson called the school to schedule an interview. His timing was perfect.

As Gunderson walked out to the family van that would take him to his interview, he thought of the troubled adolescents he had counseled while serving at the air force bases in Europe. However, he could handle high school students on the base differently than those in the States, he thought, as the base commanders always knew how to put enough pressure on active duty parents and their spouses to remind them of their responsibility for their children. Public school in California would be different. He had heard about how many schools were influenced by the Hollywood drug culture in southern California, and he didn't find the worldly lifestyle near his home to be conducive to higher academic achievement either. As he drove to the school, he prayed for divine guidance.

Pulling up to Sandpebble Charter High School was like driving onto a college campus. Gunderson was impressed with the modern architecture, the colorful beach designs, the style of the buildings, and the cleanliness of the grounds. Even though he spied a few students who were dressed immodestly, he smiled and returned a wave before parking his car in a visitors' spot.

"Hello, you must be Mr. Gunderson," said the secretary who stood behind the counter in the school's main office.

"Yes, I have an appointment with the principal at two o'clock."

"School is just about out," she said. "We have a shortened day today. I believe Principal Franklin is out on the grounds now, but he should be here in about ten minutes, if you don't mind waiting over there on the couch. I know he's expecting you."

Gunderson smiled and nodded as he walked to the blue velvet couch and sank down into it. It was the type of couch that could have easily been used as a bed, and Gunderson wondered if the principal had ever slept in it overnight. The magazine rack next to the couch contained conservative periodicals about children, school, and child-rearing. He picked one up and surveyed the images. He was happy to see traditional families portrayed in the photos.

"You must be Mr. Gunderson," boomed a voice, accompanying by an outstretched hand that floated about ten inches from his face. "I'm Principal Franklin." Gunderson rose to his feet. "Did you find a good place to park?"

"It's good to meet you, sir," Gunderson said, taking the principal's hand in a firm grip. "Yes, I found parking all right. You have a very impressive campus."

"Thank you. We have a paint crew still working on a job over by the gate. I'm glad you found a good parking spot; our seniors sometimes use the visitors' parking."

"Oh no—parking was no problem. I found a spot right out front there," he said glancing to the parking region just outside across from the customer service counter."

"Good, good. Well, come in and we'll get acquainted." He asked the secretary to hold his calls, held his office door open for Gunderson, and guided him into the tidy room like a car salesman escorting a potential buyer into a showroom.

The walls were decorated with plaques, trophies, and framed photographs of his family, trophy-winning school teams, and himself with various statesmen. Principal Franklin was tan and six feet five inches tall, but he appeared much taller in the wall photos, as he towered over everyone else. His grayish temples gave him a distinguished look, and his broad shoulders suggested that he spent considerable time outdoors.

Gunderson and Franklin settled themselves into the two straight-backed chairs that sat facing the desk. "I was pleasantly surprised when we got your call this morning," Franklin said. "We had just advertised for this new position, and I thought it might take a while before someone responded."

"The timing was right for me too," Gunderson replied. "We've only been back here in the States for about six months, and I'd been waiting for a position like this." Gunderson reached into his breast pocket and retrieved his resume, neatly folded lengthwise.

Franklin spent a minute scanning it before saying, "I see here that you have the right credentials and that you served as a Chaplain." He raised his eyebrows and looked up in saying the last part of his statement, a question now.

"That's right. My daily activities centered on family counseling, but I also worked as a substitute in social studies for the base high school. I really enjoyed it."

"My cousin runs a DOD high school on a base in Korea," Franklin said. "He says he wouldn't go back to teaching at a public school here. Says there's no rigor or discipline anymore. What do you think?"

"I can understand his perspective, but I believe that it all comes back to what's happening in the families. Overseas, families have to stay strong to adjust to the foreign culture around them. Here, there's a loss of respect for the institution of the family itself."

"I couldn't agree with you more, Mr. Gunderson. I believe it all started with the dual-career families that emerged in the 1970s—but that's all a different subject." The principal stood and walked around the desk to retrieve a thick file. "I'm gonna be direct with you, Gunderson," he continued. "Some of our kids are messed up in their heads because of drugs, and some have been so spoiled by their amateur parents that they're just as messed up. We're trying to keep a considerable number of them from dropping out, so we've been authorized to substitute certain math and social studies courses with this new home economics class. The good thing about this class is that there's a lot of room for the teacher to be creative, but we're looking for someone who can help lead them to make sound moral decisions regarding money, relationships, career paths, and things like that. It's really more like a life skills course than anything else, and we're happy that the district is allowing us teach it."

"Is that your class roster?" asked Gunderson, referring to the thick file.

"I wouldn't call it a roster yet, but these are the students we're planning to enroll. I brought it out because I wanted you to look at their profiles before making any decisions."

Franklin handed Gunderson the folder, and Gunderson gently opened it. Though the students' names had been blotted out to protect confidentiality, Gunderson felt as if he already knew some of them. He perused the first three profiles:

> Student A
> Age: 17
> Religion: Atheist
> Family History: Student's parents divorced after ten years of marriage when she was three years old. Mother was diagnosed with a personality disorder and refused treatment but won custody of the child. A restraining order has been issued against the father, who claims the mother is manipulating the children.
> Medication: Adderall for concentration.
> Criminal Background: Three arrests for public drunkenness.

Student B:

Age: 17

Religion: No Preference. Father is Muslim, mother is Catholic.

Family History: Student's parents had been living together unmarried before separating over religious differences when child was seven. Father owns a business and returns to the Middle East several times a year. Father visits with child a few times a year. Mother is employed as a manager.

Medication: Ritalin for ADHD. Child has been treated for self-mutilation and suicidal tendencies.

Criminal Background: One arrest for possession of marijuana.

Student C:

Age: 17

Religion: No preference

Family History: Child has been involved in a gang since the death of his father while on military duty as a field commander in the US Army. Mother is employed as an executive assistant in a bank. Mother says she cannot control her son, who continues to use and sell methamphetamines.

Medication: None

Criminal Background: Five arrests for possession of marijuana, physically pushing a teacher, and possession of paraphernalia to produce methamphetamines.

Gunderson flipped through the remaining files in hopes of finding students with some semblance of stability. There were a few, but the reality of most of the students' circumstances rocked him. Clearly, the home ec. course was an urgent attempt to save troubled students from dropping out of high school, dropping into the juvenile court system, or dropping dead.

"What's this one about?" he asked, holding up one student's file. "It says she's a manic depressive, but it only has her mother's name with a code next to it in the column for the father's name."

"Oh, that's Jennifer. She's doesn't know who her father is. She's going through an identity crisis of sorts in part because her father was a sperm donor who signed a confidentiality statement. She knows him only as 'donor XQU14.'"

"I was reading an article about the children of sperm donors last week," Gunderson said. "It seems quite a few go through manic depression, and there's a high rate of attempted suicide among them for some reason. A teenaged girl was suing to know the name of her biological father."

"That's right!" said, Franklin. "It was a feature in the local news. They're more likely to have mental and emotional disorders than other kids. To tell you the truth, I signed this girl up for the class after reading that story. It's too bad there's not a whole lot of data on kids like that because the sperm-donor industry isn't well regulated."

"Well," said Gunderson with a sigh, "you definitely have a unique group of kids here, but it's a worthy cause that I'd be honored to participate in."

"Good!" said Franklin, rising from his chair and extending his hands once again. "We can get you started next Monday. See the secretary outside my office, and she'll be able to get you started with the paperwork from human resources."

Gunderson shook the principal's hand and left the office, wondering if he'd made the biggest mistake of his life.

CHAPTER 4

That evening the conversation around the Gunderson dinner table was light as usual when Mrs. Gunderson floated into the room holding a tray of broiled fish filets stuffed with fresh parsley and garlic. It was her daughter Lydia's favorite dish.

"Mom, you forgot the lemon wedges," she said, gazing at the steaming plate.

"Never mind," said Malia, her older sister. "It's still good without it."

"No, no, I've already cut them up," said Mrs. Gunderson. "I just left them on the counter. Just sit tight, and I'll be right back."

Mr. Gunderson was grinning when he spoke. "Malia, Lydia chose the menu tonight so she's entitled to have it her way. Next month you can ask Mom to make another lasagna the way you like it."

"Yay! Just ask her not to put in any raisons this time," said her younger brother, Zacharias.

Mrs. Gunderson returned balancing a dish of lemon wedges in one hand and holding a water pitcher in the other. She placed them at the center of the table and sat down on her husband's right-hand side.

Keith Gunderson was smiling. "A masterpiece, Janet! Look at that tray! We need you to enter one of those competition cooking shows on TV and win $10,000."

Janet Gunderson Smiled.

"Yeah, Mom, then we could get those digital games I was showing you," said Zach. The discussion of digital games had been taboo in the Gunderson household since Keith decided to screen every game before exposing his children to them.

"Let's pray," Keith said, changing the subject. He took his wife's hand on the right and his daughter's hand on the left. Every head was inclined around the table as he spoke: "Bless us, O Lord, and these Thy gifts which we are about to receive. Make us truly grateful for Your every provision. We ask that You bless this food for the nourishment of our bodies. In Jesus' name we pray, amen."

Keith was about to scoop up a fish filet with a plastic spatula when Lydia spoke. "Daddy?" she asked, her eyes on her plate.

"Yes, Liddy?"

"Do you remember that girl I was talking about who has to sit in the front of the class because of her glasses?"

"Yes," he said, taking a bite. "Isn't her name Cathy?"

"That's the one. Well, today at the zoo she had some problems."

"What happened?"

"She stepped on a chicken."

"She what?"

Mrs. Gunderson interrupted. "The poor girl is so nearsighted that she found herself wandering away from the group, and the chaperone didn't notice that she was walking into a restricted area."

"It sounds like the chaperone dropped the ball," Keith said.

"The poor girl and the chaperone were obviously embarrassed when everyone turned around to see why the chicken was shrieking and flailing its wings," Janet replied. "Liddy, do you ever talk with that girl?"

"Sometimes, but she's kinda shy. She has a backpack like mine, and sometimes we get them mixed up so I have to show her that mine is a little different."

"Perhaps you should try to be her friend," Keith suggested. "Maybe you could invite her to church."

"Shouldn't we ask her parents first?" Malia asked.

"We could, sweetheart, but we don't know them, do we, Janet?"

"I haven't seen them at any PTA meetings," Janet replied, "but often the parents will take their kids to church if the children ask them. I'll look for her mother at the next meeting."

"And if the parents don't want to, maybe her older sister can take her," said Lydia.

"How do you know she has an older sister?" asked Malia.

"She has a picture of her in the pocket of her backpack. She's at Sandpebble Charter high school."

"Maybe I'll be able to invite the sister myself," said Keith.

All eyes were on Keith now because they were all familiar with his playful ways of introducing an announcement. The only sound was that of Zach's fork clinking against his plate as he separated his peas from his carrots until Malia asked, "Weren't you gonna tell us something, Dad?"

"Well, sure," Keith said, teasing. "I think it's your turn to do the dishes, isn't it?"

"Daaaad!" all three children chimed.

"Okay, okay, if you all insist in knowing: I start teaching at Sandpebble Charter High on Monday." Smiles and a smattering of applause circulated around the table as Keith closed his eyes and inclined his head, taking a modest bow.

"Woo-hoo! You go, Dad!" Lydia called.

Janet was grinning. "What are you teaching?" she asked.

"It's a new kind of home economics class. Get this: They want it to be taught from a Judeo-Christian perspective so the kids can learn some morals. The Catholic diocese is paying for some of it."

"But doesn't that violate the separation between church and state?" asked Malia.

"They've handled that with what's called a broad flexibility waiver. The parents had to sign a statement allowing the children to be exposed to Christian religious concepts. I'll even be able to quote from the Bible. Can you imagine that? From the look of the students' profiles, I suspect that most of them may not have had any exposure to Christian teachings."

"Wow, Dad. I wonder if Monica will be in your class," said Malia. "She's the cousin of a girl on my gymnastics team. My friend talks about her all the time—she's supposed to be smart."

"I think this class was intended for struggling students, Malia," Keith said. "I don't think she'll be there."

"Dad," asked Zach, "what's a smuggling student?"

"No, not smuggling students, Zach. Struggling students. There's a difference between struggling and smuggling." Then he added under his breath, "though I think some of these kids are capable of smuggling."

"But what's the difference?"

"Well, a struggling student has difficulty completing his assignments and making good grades—almost like how you have difficulty finishing your vegetables," he said, pointing to Zach's plate.

"I don't wanna to be a struggling student," said Zach.

"We don't want you to struggle either, dear," said Janet, scooping up a spoonful of Zach's mixed peas and carrots.

CHAPTER 5

M onday morning was overcast, as fog banks from the nearby beaches lingered in the air, reducing visibility for the early morning traffic. The administrators at Sandpebble Charter High School anticipated multiple tardy students.

Keith Gunderson arrived thirty minutes early to set up his first lesson. Janet had helped him arrange his room with youth-oriented posters and a school calendar, which were designed to be constant reminders of appropriate social behavior and encouragement to overachieve. One of the posters was a multicolored, faded image of Albert Einstein with the bold words emblazoned in the foreground: "Even Einstein asked questions." Another poster, placed just in back of the last row of student chairs, bore the images of two girls whispering and pointing to a third girl, whose face was nearly in tears. The caption read, "Gossip isn't cool. Before you judge someone, take a walk in their shoes."

He stepped back to admire the classroom, proud of himself and his family. This new position would be a new adventure, and he appreciated the high calling of teaching.

The first bell sounded on campus, and security guards outside unlocked the gates to allow the students into class. Gunderson barely had time to walk back to his desk before his door opened and a flood of students shuffled in.

"Mornin'," said one girl. "Is there a seating chart or can we sit anywhere?"

"You can sit wherever you like today," said Gunderson, "and we'll see if we'll need to have a seating chart tomorrow."

She was a ghoulish-looking young woman with hair dyed jet-black, chalky skin, and exaggerated black makeup around her eyes. Her black T-shirt and jeans highlighted her freshly polished black fingernails. Gunderson thought back to some of the student profiles and tried to place her among them, but he couldn't. The girl took her seat in the back row while others continued to stream into the room. Some appeared to be excited about being in the class, and others already had smirks of disapproval on their teenaged faces. They were an unsightly lot, a cast of characters adorned in anything but proper clothes, and Gunderson began to feel uneasy.

"Okay, class, find a seat somewhere," he said in a commanding voice. "There is no seating chart at this time, so feel free to sit anywhere."

As if on cue, one athletic-looking boy leapt across the room and sat on the lap of a blonde girl in the last row. She giggled and turned red with embarrassment.

"The teacher said I can sit anywhere I like," he said to the girl. "Ain't that right, teacher?"

"No, that's not right," said Gunderson, "and you have five seconds to find yourself a proper seat."

"It's cool," he said. Then, looking back at the girl, he added, "But I'll see you on the bus, mama." Another bell sounded and the jostling of the thirteen students in the classroom finally subsided.

Gunderson looked at them and smiled. "You students are the first of a very special program at this school," he said. "I'm so glad to teach you! My name is Mr. Gunderson, and I'm ecstatic about being here for this new course in home economics. Now, I know that your parents have all been notified about the uniqueness of our curriculum, and I'm sure that most of you know this course is designed to fulfill one of the math or social studies requirements you need, so I'd like you to just relax and—"

Before Gunderson could finish speaking, another student opened the door and swaggered into the classroom. He was the only African American student in the class. He had a tight cornrow hairstyle and wore a black T-shirt with two silver chains against his chest.

"Hey, what's up, man?" he said to Gunderson. "It's 'bout time this school hired a brutha." He suspended his hand in the air, waiting for Gunderson to meet him in a high five. Instead, Gunderson simply looked at the clownish child.

"Come on, brutha. You ain't gonna leave me hanging now?" the boy said.

"What's your name, son?" Gunderson asked.

"You can call me J.T., my brutha. What can I call you?"

"You will call me Mr. Gunderson. Now end your performance and take your seat."

"Uh oh, your voice says you're one of them Oreo-cookie bruthas."

Gunderson knew he was being tested. The class fell silent as the students waited for his next move.

"J.T., you just remain right where you are, my brutha. I'm going to make a quick phone call if you don't mind." Gunderson walked to his desk and pushed a quick-dial button. Then he pushed the loudspeaker button so the whole class could hear the phone ringing. It rang three times before someone picked it up.

"Hello?" said the female voice on the other end.

J.T.'s facial expression quickly became solemn as the class gasped.

"Mrs. Johnson, this is Keith Gunderson at Sandpebble Charter High School," said Gunderson. "Your son, J.T., arrived late today, and he seems to be having difficulty finding a seat in my classroom. I wanted to give him a chance to talk with you before I have to excuse him from class."

"Where is J.T.?" came Mrs. Johnson's annoyed voice.

"He's right here. I have you on speakerphone. He can hear you."

"J.T.!" the voice shouted over the speaker. "J.T.!"

J.T. froze. Then he looked at his classmates, most of whom were grinning.

"Yes, Ma," he said, looking down.

"Do you remember those concert tickets we were talking about last night?"

"Yeah."

"You can forget about them if I have to be called again, d'ya hear that, boy?"

"I heard it."

"All right now, baby, this is the last chance for you to good so you can graduate. Please, now, cooperate with this man!"

"All right, Ma," J.T. said in a small voice.

"Bye-bye, baby."

"Bye, Ma."

Gunderson disconnected the phone line. There was silence in the classroom until Gunderson said, "Now, have a seat—my brutha."

A few students applauded, but Gunderson held up a hand. "Now, who can tell me why I had to do that?" he said. "Is it because I like humiliating a student in front of his peers, or is there some other reason?"

The room was silent.

"Well, I'll tell you why. It's because accountability helps us stay on the right track. Accountability often means that we respect and obey those who are responsible for us because those are the people who make the greatest difference in our lives. They can reward us or take things like concert tickets away from us. All of you are accountable to your parents. This thing called accountability is crucial because it has a direct impact on issues pertaining to home economics."

The athletic-looking student raised his hand: "Mr. Gunderson," he said, "what does home economics have to do with being accountable to your parents?"

"I'm glad you asked that question. What's your name?"

"Brad."

"Okay, Brad, let me put it this way: We all make choices every day—choices to buy things, choices to say things, choices regarding how we spend our time. When we're not mindful about our accountability to others and how our decisions affect others, we often affect our families in a negative way."

"But I make decisions by myself and for myself only, and I'm not going to change that," Brad said. "So you're saying that I'm not going to be able to do anything positive because I think for myself?"

"No, not exactly. Listen, I realize that most of you are here, not because you chose it, but because your parents thought it would be beneficial for you, and you complied with it. So you don't make all your decisions exclusively for yourself, especially at your age. Even if you did, it's a dangerous thing to make decisions without being aware of your accountability to others. It's self-centered. Lack of accountability has been part of what's behind many troubles in families and even in countries."

Sitting in the second row, Theresa Jezabell Jablanski felt conflicted. She understood self-centeredness because she saw it not only in her mother but also in herself. She felt unaccountable to anyone and didn't see how her decisions affected anyone—and she didn't like that. It was lonely and depressing. She looked up to raise a question. "Sir," she said, "can I ask you a personal question?"

"As long as it's not too personal, go ahead."

"Uh, I'm Theresa by-the-way. I wanted to ask who are you accountable to?"

"That's a good question. First, let me say, I'm accountable to God—in fact, we're all accountable to Him for everything we do. Second, would be my wife and—"

"But what if you don't even believe in God?" Theresa said.

"That doesn't matter. I may not believe that I should stop at traffic lights, but I'll still get a ticket if I don't. God has set up a natural order of things to protect us, and your lack of belief in God doesn't make Him any less God. Now, I know what some of you are thinking: 'What does God or accountability have to do with home economics?' The answer is that they have everything do to with home economics because our decisions that relate to our homes have a moral basis to them, and the economics—or economy of our homes—is not just about paying the bills but about how we live together. Are you with me?"

Silence.

"Okay, what do you say we start with your textbooks? I'd like for someone to read page ten on 'The Family' for a start. J.T., would you mind reading?"

"Naw, man, I don't mind." The class tittered, and J.T. sat up straighter.

"Great."

J.T. read: "The family is the basic unit of society. Most people belong to a family and depend on the support they gain from their families. In this book you will learn 'bout the family life cycle and how new families are formed through marriage. You will learn 'bout parenting and the responsibilities that parents have. You will learn 'bout what makes a family healthy. Finally, you will learn 'bout problems in families and where to get help with problems."

"Thank you, J.T.," Gunderson said with a smile at the boy. "Now I want to ask you all a question that will require a little bit of thinking, so don't answer out loud right away. The question is this: how did the family get started? Your book says that it is the basic unit of society, and—other books say that the family is the oldest institution on this Earth. So my question is: how did this thing called family get started?"

After about thirty seconds Brad raised his hand and said, "Once a cave man saw a cave chick that he wanted, he just grabbed her by the hair, dragged her home, and they had babies. That's how the first family got made."

"Oh, please!" said the ghoulish girl. "It had to have been done by osmosis or something. Organisms must have just evolved that way."

There was another silent interlude before the blonde girl spoke up, saying, "Mr. Gunderson, we give up. Can you just tell us?"

What's your name?"

"I'm Jennifer."

"Okay, Jennifer." Gunderson pulled his top desk drawer open and took out a thick book encased in a worn brown leather cover. It was filled with multicolored sticky-notes as page markers. He opened the book and began reading: "'And God said let us make man in our own image, after our likeness, and let them have dominion over the fish of the sea, and over the fowl of the air, and over the cattle, and over all the earth and over every creeping thing that creepeth on the earth.' Chapter two, verse eighteen. 'And the Lord God said, It is not good for man to be alone, I will make him a helpmeet for him.' Verse twenty-one. 'And The Lord God caused a deep sleep to fall upon Adam, and he slept; and He took one of his ribs and closed up the flesh instead thereof, and the rib which the Lord God had taken from man, made he a woman and brought her to the man.'"

"Mr. Gunderson," said Brad, "are you kidding? You can't bring a Bible into a school to teach from it. There's a separation between church and state."

Gunderson smiled and said, "Remember that this home ec. course is being partially financed by the local Catholic diocese, and it's designed to be taught from a Judeo-Christian perspective. The separation between church and state was designed to protect the church from the state—not the other way around—and it doesn't apply to us because all of that is explained in the school's flexibility waiver. So when I explain how the first family was created as literally a match made in heaven, be mindful of this."

"Okay, Mr. Gunderson, but you've just contradicted the textbook," said Theresa Jezebel Jablanski. "J.T. read that we're going to learn how new families are formed through marriages, but there was no marriage with Adam and Eve. They just lived together without any contracts. I'm not complaining about that because I actually believe it's okay to do that."

"Actually there is no contradiction, Theresa. The problem is that we've misunderstood what marriage actually means. Marriage simply means to bring together. We have contracts today because we want our marriages to be recognized by others and our legal system, and this is the proper and wise way to go about it. But speaking about Adam and Eve, their union was in every sense a marriage because God brought them together and God Himself was their witness. Think about it: they were the only humans around. There was no legal system in place to recognize their marriage; the only other witnesses they could have had would have been gorillas and squirrels and muskrats."

The students in the back row laughed.

"Mr. Gunderson," said Brad, "we see your point. God made Adam and Eve for each other and arranged their marriage. But—"

"Oh, no, no. I didn't say that he made them for each other. I said that he arranged their marriage, and that started the first family."

"But didn't you just read that God wanted to make a helper for Adam?"

"Yes, yes. God made Eve for Adam, but he didn't make Adam for Eve. This may seem trivial but it is important because it helps us understand the nature of men and women. First Corinthians, chapter eleven says that the man was not created for the woman, but the woman for the man. So what do you think that means regarding the nature of men and women?"

"It means that's why men are abusive!" said the ghoulish girl.

"And what is your name, miss?"

"I'm Nancy."

"Nancy, it's true that many men have been abusive to women and other men, but in a family context we can see how it was in the heart of God to make Eve so Adam could have a relationship. I want all you girls to think about relationships for a moment. Healthy relationships are very important for women's well-being because that's part of why they were made. We see it in Eve, the prototype. Many girls and women are trying to achieve many types of things while denying their need to maintain healthy relationships. They're giving relationships a lower priority and wondering why they're depressed. They're doing these things because they see men doing them, and it doesn't seem to bother the men, right? We have to understand that men and women are different by design. Then we'll be able to understand more about how a functional family works."

"But aren't you simply going back to old stereotypes?" Nancy asked. "It wasn't too long ago when women weren't seen as equal and had to suffer abuse. Now you're saying again that we're not equal."

"Oh, no, no, not for a moment. I'll have to ask my wife to come in one day and talk about that. Men and women are definitely equal in the sight of God—the value of a human soul is equal across the board—but the confusion comes in when we think that equality means sameness. Being equal doesn't mean being the same. Men and women are not interchangeable in everything like some might want you to believe."

"Wait up!" J.T. said. "You said a lot 'bout Eve, but what 'bout Adam? Okay, Eve was made for him. I'm cool with that because he didn't have nothing but animals around, which to me is a little freaky."

"Right, and you young men really need to understand this part. Before Adam had a relationship with Eve, he had a relationship with God Himself. The Bible says that God put him in the garden to work it and that He talked to him about what he could and could not eat, but I want you to look at the progression of things that were in place before Eve was brought to him for marriage. First Adam had a relationship with God; he walked with Him and communicated with Him. Then God gave Adam a job; he had to take care of the land, name the animals, and so on. Finally, when Adam was ready, God brought him a wife that Adam could provide for and protect and love to glorify God. But do you see the progression? First he knew God, then he knew what God wanted him to do with his life, and only then did God bring him a woman and they became a family."

"You see," Gunderson continued, "there is something divine about this order that stabilizes the building of families. But what are men doing today? They want to get married first. They have no idea about what their calling in life is and no knowledge of God, but they want to assume the responsibility of leading a home. Their priorities are out of order. And many aren't even thinking of providing or protecting anymore. They want to be provided for and protected! This is the beginning of instability in families, and it starts with the decisions of the male, just as the first family started with Adam's decision to marry Eve, rather than uniting with, say, one of the muskrats." Gunderson smiled again.

Jennifer was provoked. Her hand shot up. "Sir," she said, "you've been talking a lot about things I've never thought about, but there are so many single-parent homes now that I have to ask: Is the presence of a father really all that important in the home today?"

"Jennifer, it's absolutely imperative that children be raised by a mother and father in order to have a healthy, balanced upbringing, but it is probably more important now for kids to be connected with their fathers than it might have ever been. He's the head. He brings order and identity to the family."

"But how does he bring identity?" Jennifer asked.

"Well, let's think for a minute. For a start, he gives us a name. You all realize that you carry your father's last name, don't you?"

Nancy spoke up, "No, not me. I have my mother's maiden name."

"Well, Nancy, where did your mother's maiden name come from?"

"It's from my mother. It was her name before she got married."

"All right, but where did she get it?"

J.T. spoke up. "She got it from her own daddy!"

Nancy nodded.

"Okay, Nancy, you get my point?" Gunderson said. "Family names come from males. Your mother's maiden name is actually your grandfather's family name, so the male connection is still there. But that's just one way in which our fathers pass an identity on to us. Did you know that most males end up doing a type of work that is very closely related to or exactly the same type of work their fathers did? Finally, here's something that I'm sure none of you have thought of: God designed it so your very gender identity would be determined by your father."

Jennifer now knew what he was talking about and blurted out, "Oh, I know about that! It's true because men have XY chromosomes, and women have XX chromosomes."

"Wow, that's good Jennifer," Gunderson said with a grin. "Could you explain more about this to the class?"

"Okay, well, when a mother's egg is fertilized by a sperm, the father provides one of his chromosomes. Since women only have two Xs, her contribution can only be an X chromosome. But since the father can provide an X or a Y, his chromosome makes the difference in whether the baby will be either XY or XX, which makes it a boy or a girl."

The class mumbled amongst themselves as Jennifer beamed.

The class continued in an open-forum discussion about family for another forty-five, minutes and every student was engaged, respecting Gunderson's teaching methodology and his use of the Bible.

CHAPTER 6

Jennifer had four homework assignments to complete, but that was the farthest thing from her mind. Her mother had to leave her by herself overnight in order to assist in an executive team presentation at the convention center. These conventions were held at least three times a year, so Jennifer knew her mother would call from the hotel around ten o'clock.

After the discussion in home ec. about family and relationships, Jennifer decided to take a chance on establishing a relationship with her father. She had carried the burden of questions for over a year now, and it was time to do something about it. Who was she? Why was she born? Who was her father? Why didn't her mother insist on meeting him at least once before she accepted the sperm donation? The hospital could give Jennifer only a faceless, nameless code: he was XQU14, which in her mind made him no different from an imported automobile part. What did he look like? Would he approve of who she was?

Jennifer sat down in front of her computer, teary-eyed, and opened a social networking site to the search engine. She entered her father's only identity, XQU14, in hopes that something would come up. She prayed and clicked enter. Pages of information rolled by in a blur until she stopped at one page:

Name: Kevin

Place of Birth: Lexington, Missouri

Age: 17

Hobbies: Riding horses, skiing, paintballing

Jennifer's screen was still in message mode, so she couldn't see any photos yet, but she thought about whether to make contact with this person who was associated with the code XQU14. Who was he? He was only seventeen. She had heard about the many scams on the network site and how predators were always coming up with new techniques. The thought of making contact with Kevin from Missouri frightened her; it reminded her of how horrified she felt when her mother's boyfriend made advances toward her at the picnic. But it was time to venture out, time at least to make an effort. The emptiness that she felt was real, and she knew that no other relationship could fill it.

She began to type:

> Hello. My name is Jennifer, and I'm looking for my father. I've never met him, and I would very much like to. He was a sperm donor, and his code is XQU14. Please tell me if you can help me.

> She clicked, and the message was sent to Kevin. Then the telephone rang.

"Hello, sweetie. This is Kay," the voice said when Jennifer picked up.

"Oh, hi, Mom."

"Did you get my message about the convention?"

"What message?"

"I left it on your dresser. I'm spending the night at the hotel, but I'll be back tomorrow afternoon."

"I knew about it anyway because we talked about it last week."

"Okay, sweetie, I just thought I'd call to make sure everything is all right."

"Everything's fine, Mom."

"Make sure you set the house alarm before you go to bed, okay?"

"Okay, Mom."

"And, sweetie, you're not to have any guests over while I'm out, all right?"

"Got it, Mom."

"Okay. I love you."

"Okay, Mom. Bye." She hung up.

The dark, silent stillness in her bedroom reflected the emptiness that lingered in Jennifer's troubled soul. She waited for a response to her message, knowing that sometimes it took days for network members even to take notice, but she hung on. She looked down at her arms in shame at the zebra-patterned traces of cutting and self-embedding. Months of psychotherapy had been helpful only in that they allowed her to focus her attention on something besides herself, as negative thoughts of worthlessness were temporarily pushed aside to explore behavioral modification techniques and theories, and the enjoyment of some laughter, but the emptiness always returned. At least for now, however, she didn't feel like cutting herself.

Her computer screen flickered and she jumped. Her message box blinked a message from Kevin. She took a breath and clicked on it:

> Jennifer, I just got your message. I can't believe this. Thank God you found me! I don't know anything about you, but you're my half-sister. I've advertised our father's code name for two months, hoping to get some feedback, and you're the second person to show up. I'm looking to meet him myself, but at least I know I have a sister now. I live in Missouri. It would be great to talk. This feels so weird! Anyway, I'll let you in through my friends inbox so we talk live and see each other. Waiting for your response.

Jennifer hesitated. She wished she wasn't alone and thought about calling her mother but decided against it, not being sure what she might think. She exhaled audibly, realizing she'd been holding her breath, and composed a response:

> Hi, Kevin. Before I log on as a friend, I have to be sure that that is real. How do I know you're not some predator or something? If you are a predator, please think about what you're doing. You're playing with someone's life here. I've been waiting too long to be played around with!

She clicked the send button, and her message was gone. Within thirty seconds Kevin replied:

> Jennifer, I understand your anxiety, but this is not a joke. I've waited a long time too. I learned about my sperm-donor dad only last summer. I grew up thinking that he had been killed in Iraq because that's what my mother told me, but last summer she finally let the cat out of the bag. She doesn't know much about him but

said that he was a Rhodes scholar. Anyway, we can talk more about him. You'll just have to trust me.

Jennifer thought. She recalled the times when her gut feeling was right about new contacts and the times she had ignored her gut feelings and suffered the consequences. There was something undeniably sincere about this. How could a predator have access to her father's identity code anyway? She crossed her fingers and decided to log on as a friend in the hopes of interacting with him in a live, face-to-face conversation. She clicked her mouse and the screen jumped and flashed.

They were face to face. The two adolescents stared at each other blankly for what seemed an eternity without saying a word. They had the same nose and the same folds in their foreheads just above their eyes. Her face was nearly identical to his.

CHAPTER 7

"Mmmmm," Zach intoned as his mother passed him a dish of steamy macaroni and cheese. His turn to choose the menu had finally come that evening, and he had been thinking about macaroni and cheese all afternoon.

"Zach, move your water glass over so I can put this on your placemat," said his mother.

Zach slid his water glass six inches to the right, causing some of his drink to spill.

"Okay, can we pray, Dad?" Lydia said. "I don't think Zach will be able to maintain his composure any longer." Zach snickered.

"Okay," Keith Gunderson said. "Let's pray. Our heavenly Father, make us truly thankful for this food. Please bless it for our nourishment, and bless our fellowship at the table. In Jesus' name we pray, amen."

The Gunderson household always looked forward to their evening meals together, especially on Friday nights, as it was a time to get excited about the weekend. Malia and Lydia were always relieved to get a break from their homework, Zach always looked forward to doing something special with his father on Saturday afternoons, and Janet Gunderson looked forward to grocery shopping with her daughters and some of the women from her church prayer group. Somehow grocery shopping was fun for her girls when mothers from the church came along with their own teen daughters.

Janet was cutting up her broccoli when she said, "Keith, Barbara told me that she saw your letter to the editor in the paper."

"She did? Wow, it's been two weeks. I thought they wouldn't publish it."

"Why not?"

"Well, you know how people are. Conservative viewpoints rarely get any publicity in the press these days."

"It opened up a few eyes for some of the women at the weekly prayer group," Janet continued. "We've decided to add all of our children to the prayer list for Wednesday afternoons. I couldn't get them to stop talking about your letter."

"Why are they putting us on their prayer list, Mom?" asked Malia.

"Honey, we just want to be sure you're all covered in prayer while you're at school. Kids are involved in so many adult like issues that they don't have the maturity level to deal with. And there's been an increase in violence in public schools. We never heard about kids bringing guns to school in Europe, but it's a reality here so we need to keep you all in constant prayer."

"Let's just do homeschooling, Mom!" said Zach.

Janet's eyes opened wide in surprise before she responded with "I'm open to however the Lord wants to lead us in that, but your father and I decided before we left Europe to enroll you all in public schools. You just don't jump into something like home schooling that without prayer and guidance first."

"Talking about adult issues," said Gunderson, changing the subject. "Remember that one girl I was talking about who never knew her father?"

"You mean the child who sits in the back of the class and whose father was sperm donor?"

"That's her. Yesterday she told me she met someone online who's a part of her family on her father's side—her half brother."

"You mean they're brother and sister, and they've never met before?" gasped Lydia between sips of fruit juice.

"That's right, they've never met. I have a funny feeling about this girl, and I want us all to keep her in prayer. Her name is Jennifer. All her life she's wanted to know who her father is, and she's trying to do something so she can meet him. I guess our class discussions about the family have made her reflect on her own family tree."

"Mom, what's a sperm donor?" inquired Zach.

"Uh, honey, it just means that she has never known her father since the time when she was born. Eat your vegetables." Janet turned to Keith and asked, "What's her mother saying about all of this?"

"I don't know if her mother even knows about it. Jennifer is pretty introverted sometimes. She keeps everything wrapped up inside."

"Kinda like me, Dad?" asked Lydia.

"No, not really. You understand that God wants us to be transparent, to live in the open, unashamed. When we have a problem, we talk to

Him and ask for prayer support from others. The kids at school don't understand these things."

"Raising children was never intended to be done without God's help," said Janet.

"Oh that reminds me!" Keith said, raising an eyebrow and glancing at his wife. "We'll be starting the section on child-raising this Monday. The class is all ready to hear from our excellent guest speaker on the subject."

"Mom, are you gonna talk to Dad's class?" asked Lydia.

"It'll be more of an informal chat about raising children," Janet said. "I just hope they'll listen to me."

"Mom's gonna teach! Mom's gonna teach!" Malia cheered in playful support. "Woo-hoo! You go, Mom! I wish I could be there!"

"You will be there, honey, in every sentence. I'm going to talk about all of you and our experiences bringing you up and how the Lord spared us from our mistakes."

"Tell 'em about how I almost electrocuted myself in the bathtub using Dad's laptop," Zach said cheerfully. "I'll bet they'll listen to you after that."

"No, please, Mom, don't tell that story," said Malia. "I might know some of those girls, and they'll think that we're all from another planet or something if you tell them how your son used a laptop to scuba dive in the bathtub."

Janet chuckled at her children. "Every family has stories like that, Malia. That's nothing to be embarrassed about. But I won't be sharing those types of stories anyway. Besides, it's hard to keep the attention of teenagers these days. Maybe I should bring something like our family photo album to help keep their attention."

"No, Mom, please don't!" Lydia shrieked, and Malia and Zach chimed in with her. "They'll be able to see all of those nude bubble-bath photos," continued Lydia, "aren't those pictures only meant for the family?" Janet thought for a moment.

"Mom, I think I can help here," said Malia in a serious voice. "There's something you have right here in this house that will captivate your audience, especially the girls." Malia stood up and whispered something in her mother's ear. Janet's eyes grew large, seeming almost to sparkle. Then a warm smile swept across her face.

CHAPTER 8

As usual, the hallway chatter did not subside after the first bell of the first period at Sandpebble Charter High School. Students lingered around their lockers to gossip about the weekend football game and the brief after-game party at someone's house. No one noticed Janet Gunderson as she slipped through the throngs of gum-smacking teens, picking up tidbits from their conversations. She had arrived early enough to set up her husband's classroom but then slipped out into the hallway.

Though she had made it back to Gunderson's room before the warning bell, on an impulse she decided to lock the door to allow a line to form outside. She wanted all the students to walk in together, rather than having them stagger in piecemeal.

Standing patiently near the door, Janet heard scrambling outside and a tapping on the door. She could hear that the male students were excited about the apparent possibility of the class's being cancelled. Once only two minutes remained before the tardy bell, she decided that there was a large enough group to let in.

"Good morning, class," she said, opening the door with a brilliant smile. "I'm Mrs. Gunderson. Please come in. My husband has told me all about you."

The first three girls in the doorway smiled at Janet and nodded hello as they walked past her, but then they stopped and gasped as they saw the incongruous item suspended from the ceiling. More students behind them began to shove in but also halted in shock after noticing the item.

A boy shouted, "What's that thing doing there?"

Then a girl exclaimed, "That's awesome!"

A bottleneck of students formed at the doorway as the tardy bell rang, and the students who had been waiting for the crowd inside to dissipate became anxious. "Let's go, dudes, keep moving," a boy mumbled, forcing his way through, but then he also stopped to gaze at the item hanging just over their heads.

Principal Franklin, completing his rounds of collecting tardy students for the first period at this time, had forgotten that Janet was scheduled to be a guest speaker that morning and found it unusual that Gunderson's door remained open with unsettled students inside. He walked briskly to the room and stood in the doorway.

"Good morning," said Janet. "You must be Principal Franklin."

"Why, yes," he said, stepping inside, "I'm sorry. I forgot that you would be taking Gunderson's morning class, and when I saw his door still opened I thought ..."

He stopped in midsentence, flabbergasted at the sight before him as he gazed upward. Some students began to chuckle as they began taking their seats.

The principal smiled. "Well, that's one of the most beautiful sights I've seen in a long time," he said. "I assume it's yours?"

Janet smiled and nodded. Then she moved to stand just beneath it. It was a finely manufactured vanilla silk wedding gown with ornate rhinestone-studded embroidery around the neckline and sleeves. The flowing satin train was six feet long with handmade pearl-implanted designs on the outer edges. It was a wedding gown fit for royalty.

"I think I can see where you might be going with this," said the principal, still grinning. "Have a fun class and I'll get with you later." He stepped out and closed the door behind him.

Janet allowed the class to settle down in their seats. That expensive wedding gown had to be a warm-up to something big, and they were filled with anticipation. With the exception of one, all of the girls were starry-eyed over the dress, clearly picturing themselves wearing it. It was Theresa Jezabell Jablonski who was frowning and rolling her eyes.

"You are all beginning your studies on child-raising this week, is that right?" asked Janet.

The students nodded.

"Great! I hoped that I hadn't been mistaken. Well, to tell you the truth, the reason I brought my wedding gown in was to illustrate where good parenting begins. This might seem a little hokey at first, but I want you to take this very seriously, especially you girls, as the best child-raising begins with a good marriage. Statistics show that more than 90 percent of you in this class will marry someday, and most of you who marry will have children. As I look at all of your lovely faces, I can see traces of several ethnicities of various cultures, but I want you to think about another type of culture—a home culture. No matter what your ethnic culture is, each home has its own subculture. It's the way the family lives and delicately grows together. And the foundation of that subculture rests upon the marriage between the father and mother."

Theresa Jezabell Jablanski's hand shot up. A look of disapproval on her face, she was not buying any of it. "Mrs. Gunderson," she said, "our book talks about the benefits of daycare to relieve parents of the old-fashioned child-raising ways of the last century. Do you think that what you're saying really applies to us now?"

"I'm sorry," Janet said, "but I don't know your name. Are you Nancy?"

"No, I'm Theresa." Theresa raised a suspicious, penciled eyebrow and glanced at Nancy.

"I'm sorry. It's nice to meet you, Theresa. You raise an interesting perspective on daycare centers. It's true that over the last thirty years or so daycare has become a mainstream alternative to raising infants in a home environment until they reach school age. Some of these centers offer very sophisticated services and have helped out quite a few mothers, but we must be very careful when we talk about the best way to raise children. Some daycare centers are better than others, but that really matters less than the issue of a growing child being constantly separated from his or her mother during the early years of life. And I know of some mothers who have put their kids in daycare as early as two months after their birth."

"So what?" Theresa said. "What does it matter? The kid will never remember anyway."

"Oh, no, no. I'm afraid you're wrong on that," said Janet. "Listen, I'm going to be blunt about this because I know you kids are not getting the whole truth from the pop culture and media people on television, and most of you probably rely on the media for current issues. After a baby is born it's crucial for him or her to fall in love with his or her mother. Did you hear that? They have to connect really well in the first seven months of life or the baby can develop some real difficulties and behavioral problems."

"It works this way," she continued. "When a baby is separated from his or her mother, there is an increase of a stress hormone called cortisol in his or her body. If this hormone is constantly elevated in the body for a prolonged period, the development of the baby's brain can be affected, as this hormone can be like acid for a developing brain. We all know that stress is a killer for adults; well, it can do quite a bit of damage to developing kids too. If you ever take a walk through some of these daycare centers, what do you see: children sitting in large groups, crying all by themselves; no one picking them up to cuddle them; some crying because they've been in wet diapers for too long. Most just want their mommies. It is a sad sight. It's no wonder that many of these children become slow learners and socially aloof at school."

Brad raised his hand. "So are you just a stay-at-home mom," he asked, "or do you work?"

Janet laughed. "I have one of the hardest and most important jobs in the world," she said. "I'm a homemaker and a home-keeper. I also work as a pharmacist part-time while my children are at school, but that's my easy second job."

"So, you went to college to work in a pharmacy?" Brad asked.

"Oh, yes. Before I was married, I was a regional manager for a chain of pharmacies. It's a very rewarding field, but I cut back on my hours when I started having children."

"But pharmacists get a lot of money; you could be making bank!" he said, clapping a hand to his forehead.

"I'm sorry, what is your name?"

"I'm Brad."

"Brad, making bank today cannot compare with the dividends of raising well-balanced, godly children for tomorrow. My husband is a good provider for our family, and I'm the chief caretaker of the children. These are God's biblical roles."

Most of the class was staring at her with their mouths open, and Janet realized that what she was saying must have sounded like a foreign language to most of them. None of them had ever heard a modern woman talk this way.

"Listen," she said, "I know that a lot of these things may be difficult to relate to at your age, but one has to understand the importance of sacrificing for others in order to appreciate what I'm saying, okay? Good parenting will require sacrificing what you want for what's best for the family. And, girls, you must never forget that, no matter how much education or career opportunities you get, the highest calling for any woman is motherhood. Nothing can be more important than bringing a new living soul into this world—nothing!"

Nancy spoke up. "Okay," she said, "but you had a husband with a job good enough to allow you to be able to raise your children at home. Nowadays you need two incomes unless you wanna live without ever traveling or having fun."

"That's another half-truth, I'm afraid. If they sacrificed, most married mothers would be able to stay home without too much loss. In fact, many could come out slightly ahead because they wouldn't have to pay those astronomical daycare bills. The question is more about priorities—about what's important."

"Now," she continued, "you made an excellent point about the husbands. Yes, their role is to be the primary provider for the family, but too many men are falling short in filling this role. Many have good jobs, but they still expect their wives to work outside the home and to do all of the cleaning up inside too, which is sure to physically and emotionally drain her, no matter how tough an image she's trying to portray. Now, I don't completely agree with the idea of these stay-at-home dads because this unbiblical role change causes more confusion for the children, but I'm going to tell you what I tell my own daughters: don't waste your single years with immature, lazy, passive men who don't understand their role. My heart goes out to so many women—and we have some in our church—who have husbands at home that won't assume their proper roles. I don't mean for this to sound disrespectful toward men, because, girls, you will need to show your husband respect as the leader. But the reality is that many of these men are the way they are because they never had a responsible father to teach them how to assume their role. Many of these guys were from single-parent homes headed by unmarried mothers who tried to do the best they could, but a woman cannot teach a man how to be a man, and they will usually resent their mothers for even trying."

Nancy blurted out without raising her hand, "My brother is like that with my mom," she said. "She tries so hard to do 'guy things' with him, but they always get into trivial arguments. Then my brother gets stressed out and goes to smoke marijuana with his friends."

"Nancy, your brother is coming to manhood. He's going to want to lead and run the show now, and the last thing he wants is his mom trying to be like one of the guys to him. It's unnatural. What he should be learning is how to treat her like a lady. He should be opening the door for her and taking her out to dinner sometimes. Some women in our church let their sons pay the monthly bills and make small leadership decisions for the family, and when they take their mothers out to a restaurant, they pay the bill. That's what they need."

"You see," she continued, "men have changed over the last forty years largely because of a disconnect with their own fathers. They are struggling more academically and emotionally today. Did you know that 40 percent of children today are raised without fathers? And a young man's expectations of you girls may be problematic because of all of this. You see, that's why I said that the foundation for the home's culture is based upon a good marriage between a father and a mother who understand their own roles."

J.T. fidgeted in his seat and quietly shook his head in disapproval. Only three of his classmates knew that he was the likely father of an illegitimate child born to a high school junior just four days ago. The girl had been an A+ student but dropped out.

"You're J.T., aren't you?" asked Janet.

"Yeah."

"You're shaking your head. Would you like to say something?"

"Nah, not really. I mean, it all just seems like too much to ask of a dude. If women have been doing all this fighting to be equal, then let 'em work and raise the kids too. I mean, I don't wanna be the one to hold them back."

"You're copping out, J.T."

"I'm what?"

"You're copping out. You don't want the responsibility, and that's your choice. But just don't father any children with that attitude. Do you realize that a minority male child from a single-mother home statistically has a better chance of winding up in prison than he has of going to college?"

J.T. looked down.

"Young men," Janet said, looking at each boy in the room in turn, "women never intended to be considered your equal, okay? You have to remember that women are emotional, and what they say is not always what they mean. What they really want is to be valued as equals, and basically just want to be loved. Now, girls, I want to tell you, don't waste your life trying to prove something that cannot be proven. Do you hear what I'm saying? This is a slave mentality. You cannot be free and at the same time always feel that you have to prove something to somebody. Your future husband is not meant to be a competitor. As I reflect on the many women I've helped counsel in the church, without a doubt the happiest ones are the ones who admire their husbands. Did you know that the Bible says that the wife should admire her husband? It's there for a reason, girls!"

Jennifer spoke up. "Mrs. Gunderson," she asked, "why are you so passionate about all of this? I appreciate your coming to speak to us and all, and you've said some things that have really challenged my thinking—I know I would be different today if I had been brought up in the way you've been describing—but we're only seventeen years old. I mean, I know we have to know these things to pass this course, but no one is really thinking about marriage and raising kids now."

Janet was silent. Then she turned her head to look at the wedding dress, still suspended from the ceiling. Tears began to well up in her eyes, but she brushed them away before they could spill down her face.

"You've asked me why these matters are so important to me. I'll tell you why: Because I was like some of you girls, and I almost missed out. I was doing all of the right things. I kept myself pure—yes, I was a virgin, and I'm a big advocate for that. I got my high school diploma and I entered college, but I found myself on a treadmill. I was smart, and everybody kept telling me to pursue my goals for higher education and a great career, and that's what I did. But what was truly in my heart was the desire to build a home for a family."

"Many young women are in this predicament today," she continued. "They don't feel respected for wanting to be a homemaker or raise children, so some of them stay on the treadmill and try to look successful on the outside while on the inside they're dying. For many, time runs out, and they find themselves alone or they try to live a younger woman's lifestyle, which doesn't really work. I don't want that for my daughters. You see, we spend twelve years getting a formal education in order to go to college and get a good job, but later you'll find out that life is about a great deal more than getting a job. It's about family, relationships, leaving a legacy for children, and growing in your purpose. But too few are taught how to achieve these goals. Too few are taught how your character today is going to help make a destiny for you tomorrow."

"But why go to school or college then?" interjected Theresa.

"Going to school and college are good things because they'll help you find your purpose and afford you opportunities to grow and be exercised in them. With a good education you'll be able to serve others by using your gifts and talents in a very meaningful way. But girls, your purpose will change once you get married—and it'll change again when you have children."

The students were quiet, even somber. Clearly, they were not used to adults' being so transparent with them. Janet could see that they sensed her sincerity and that they simply did not know how to respond to it.

Leaning back in his chair, Brad broke the ice. He raised his hand and said, "Mrs. Gunderson, I'd just like to know what you meant by how us guys need to value our girlfriends as equal when they aren't. Isn't that what you said?"

"Naw, man," interrupted J.T. "She said you have to treat all of your girlfriends equally!"

This prompted a burst laughter among the boys and protests from the girls. A few balled-up pieces of paper flew J.T.'s way.

Janet smiled and waited a moment before responding.

"Brad," she said, "what's your favorite kind of car?"

"My favorite car? That would be an all-wheel-drive 300 horsepower Humvee H2." He turned to J.T. and exchanged a high five.

"All right, how much does one of those cost?"

"The one I like costs around $50,000."

Janet walked to the blackboard on the side wall, picked up a piece of chalk, and sketched an impressive outline of a Humvee. Then she drew in the details of the windshield, the tire rims, and back section.

"Hey, Mrs. Gunderson, that's pretty good!" said Brad.

"Thank you, Brad," she replied. "My minor was art in undergraduate school. Now, did I miss anything?"

"No, that looks like my Humvee!"

"You ain't got no Humvee, man!" said J.T.

"All right, it's the one I'm gonna get if I finish college," said Brad.

"Okay, boys," said Janet, bringing them to focus. "What makes this car so special?"

"What makes it special?" Brad said, placing his palms flat on the desk. "It's just the bomb! You can go through rough terrain without getting stuck in the mud, and with the 300 horsepower engine it'll go pretty fast anywhere. The all-wheel-drive means that it'll probably do all right in snow, mud, or sand, and I can even haul a trailer. There's just a lot you can do with it."

"Okay, I got it. Thanks, Brad. Now I want you to try to guess what I'm drawing over here." Janet used the chalk to draw a dividing line on the board. The Humvee remained on the left side, and she drew another type of vehicle on the right. It was smaller and sleek, curvaceous and flashy. It wasn't long before a student blurted out, "That's a Mustang!"

"No, not quite," said Janet.

"Oh, I know that car," said Nancy. "My aunt has one. It's a Mercedes coupe, class, E."

"Very good," said Janet, adding the finishing touch of the Mercedes trademark symbol on the front. "How does your aunt use this car, Nancy?"

"Well, that's a coupe, and hers is a convertible. We like to let the top down to joyride along the coast. It's a smooth car! Most times you can't even tell that the engine is running!"

"I see," said Janet. "Now I want you guys to notice something here, and it's crucial that you get this point. Brad said that the Humvee here on the left costs around $50,000. But take a look at this."

She used a piece of colored chalk to write "$50,000" under the Humvee and then wrote the same figure underneath the Mercedes. The class watched, anticipating an explanation.

"So they're the same price?" someone asked.

"Yes," said Janet, "but they're not just the same price; they each have the same value. But we'll get back to that. Here's the important part: Brad, what do you think would happen to this Mercedes coupe if you treated it like you want to treat your Humvee?"

"It'd be messed up."

"Why is that?"

"Because it wasn't designed to do that stuff."

"How long do you think it would take to mess it up?"

"I dunno. Depends how rough you use it, I guess."

"For a while you could probably get away with driving up rough terrain and hauling heavy loads, but you would cut its life short. For a certain time it may appear to be doing the job well, but—you're right—it definitely wouldn't last as long as it would if you didn't drive it that way. Now, here's the other question: what would happen if I decided to use the Humvee in the way you would use the Mercedes coup?"

"Nothin' would happen," said J.T.

"Why not?"

"Because you're not pushing it. You're wasting your money if you use it like the Mercedes."

"Would that be because the Humvee would not be reaching its potential?"

"Yeah," said J.T.

"You guys are sharp! Now let's get back to Brad's question. You see here that these two vehicles are completely different by design, but they have the same value. Though they were made differently, they have equal value. Young men, you were made uniquely by design. God did it that way. Young ladies, you were made uniquely by design too, and you have the same value as the young men. Your differences don't create a difference in value, only in function!"

"Girls," she continued, "if you want to use your bodies in the way that men do, for a while it might look like nothing's happening, but wait a while, and your body will start to tell you things. The stress will start to take a toll. When you start experiencing signs of osteoporosis, you'll want to be careful how you work out in the gym. When your bones start to suffer stress fractures like the female Marine recruit in the news who was discharged from physical training, your body will be trying to tell you something, so listen to it."

Mrs. Gunderson took a breath. "How is it that young women in this culture believe they can do the same things that young men do without suffering consequences later? Even young girls on soccer teams are beginning to have concussion problems from head-butting the ball because their skulls are not as thick as the boys' skulls. If they used a lighter ball, it would be all right, but that would mean we'd have to admit that there's a difference between boys and girls. People don't want to do that. But the Bible says that men are to give honor to women as a weaker vessel. Do you hear that, boys? Taking advantage of women in any way makes you less of a man because you're supposed to protect, provide for, and give honor to women."

"So I guess we know what you think about putting women in front-line combat roles," said Theresa.

"Well, I'd like for you to look into these things yourself, as you won't get a full picture from the media or politics. You have to use some critical thinking on your own. You must know by now that my husband was a chaplain in the military and sometimes had to counsel active duty members. He's heard about all kinds of post-traumatic stress disorders today from the wars in the Middle East, and studies are already showing how the rates of suicide for women increase significantly when they've been exposed to war zones."

"But what do you think might happen," she continued, "if you have women on the front line getting captured by the enemy? What do you think these men are going to do with them? I tell you one thing: they're not going to just lock them up for questioning like they do male prisoners. No way. Remember: these men have been fighting for months. They've been away from their own wives for an extended period, and they're hostile. Girls, my husband and I have talked to many young women about their vulnerabilities during war, and we've heard things that I wouldn't dare share with you today. But you can be sure about this: civilian women and children have always been high on the casualty list during wars, and if they're going to put women on the front lines to fight an all-male enemy, we'd better prepare for not only increased female casualties but post-traumatic stress disorders like we have never seen before."

CHAPTER 9

It was a popular R & B tune by a 1980s one-hit-wonder band, and the synthesized music created a mellow background that drowned out the clatter of plates and social chatter at the beach café—the perfect spot for the encounter. Jennifer had agreed to meet her half-brother Kevin on a Saturday because she felt safer waiting in a crowded place during a busy time for the business. Her protective friend Debby went along to watch her inconspicuously from a corner table. It was an encounter that Jennifer had been anticipating now for two months, although Kevin had told his mother he would be spending the weekend with a friend in Missouri, he would be nearly two thousand miles away.

"What if he doesn't come?" asked Jennifer, twisting her napkin in damp hands.

"What do you mean?"

"What if he changed his mind? What if he's not interested?"

"Jenny, this isn't a blind date! He's your brother—or at least he thinks he is. Didn't he give you the flight number and everything?"

"Yeah."

"All right then. If everything goes according to schedule, he should be here in thirty minutes."

"Okay, but, Debby?"

"Yeah?"

"Why am I scared? I mean, we've talked about this for two months, but now I'm not sure I want to go through with it."

"Go through with what? You're just meeting your sperm-donor half-brother, for goodness sake. It's not like he's going to expect anything from you. He's just trying to piece his own identity together, and he has to start with you."

"I guess you're right. You know, he said he had a surprise to share with me, and I just can't imagine what that's all about."

"Maybe this is all just a well-planed joke by your ex-boyfriend, and he'll walk in here with your mother."

"Oh, thanks for that thought!"

"Listen, I'm gonna take that corner table over there. I'll just sit there with a magazine and keep an eye on you. If he stands up and starts to choke you or something, I'll scream for security."

"You've always been so reassuring," said Jennifer with a wan smile.

Debby walked to the corner table, a small, round table with an attached reading lamp near a window, designed for a single patron. She sat down, ordered a cappuccino, and opened a magazine, where she found a full-page advertisement about long-distance air travel. She raised the magazine over her head to show Jennifer, giddily pointing to the picture of a DC-10 aircraft in flight and giving a thumbs-up.

Embarrassed by her antics, Jennifer turned her head and wondered whether she had done the right thing in asking Debby to come along. An unsteady flow of patrons streamed into the café in groups of two and three wearing sandals and swimwear. Every so often Debby glanced at the patrons through the window as they approached the café from the beach until she saw one who, dressed in khaki pants and a navy-blue sports shirt, looked like a tourist. He had wavy chestnut-brown hair that spilled over the top of his sunglasses and was carrying a backpack over his shoulder and was looking intently at the outside of the building. As he stood in front of the café door, he lifted his sunglasses. Then he smiled—it was Jennifer's own smile.

By this time the crowd inside had grown large enough to block Debby's view of Jennifer's table. She thus stood up on her tiptoes for greater visibility, knocking over her cup of cappuccino.

"Jen, I think this is him!" she shouted from across the room. "He's coming in!" Her voice, however, was drowned by the increasing crescendo of music and social chatter.

Kevin walked inside cautiously and stopped before heading toward the dining area.

"Hi! Table for one?" asked a waitress.

"Yes, ma'am. I mean no. I'm supposed to be meeting someone here."

"Do you know if you're party's already here?"

"She should be. Could I just have a quick look to see if she's here?"

"Why, sure, go right ahead—but if they're not here yet, we'll see if we can get you a table for two."

"Thank you."

The café reminded Kevin of a popular television series about California beach life—everyone appeared to be wearing some colorful variation of a Hawaiian shirt. No one in Missouri ever wore clothes like this, and most of the girls back home wouldn't fit in the popular bikini skirts he saw everywhere. He strolled up and down the café's main aisle, catching glimpses of the people who sat at the booths and tables. Jennifer had told him she would probably be wearing a pink windbreaker, but there was not one in sight.

"Your party's not here yet?" asked the waitress, who caught up with him after delivering a sandwich to a nearby booth.

"No, I guess not. Could I just sit here and wait?" He pointed to an empty table, where a half-filled cup of herbal tea had been left behind.

"I'm sorry. I'm afraid this one is still taken. I think the customer went to the ladies' room and should probably return any moment."

Jennifer was just returning from the ladies' room when she spotted the waitress from behind talking to a man. She knew she might be at risk of losing her table and quickly walked over to acknowledge the waitress and defend her spot.

"I'm sorry," she said to the waitress, "I had to slip away momentarily to—"

When Kevin turned around, he noticed her pink windbreaker before looking at her face. He lifted his sunglasses.

"Jenny?" he asked with a broad smile.

Jennifer smiled back. "Hi, Kevin," she said, extending her hand.

"I can see that your party is here now, sir," said the waitress with a smile. "Can I get you something to drink?"

"I'll have a cappuccino please," he said, sitting down. "How about you, miss? More tea?"

"Yes, please," said Jennifer.

Kevin shook her hand and sat down across from her, neither one sure of what to say.

"This place is great," Kevin said, looking around at the café. "Do you know that it's my first time seeing the ocean from a beach? Now I know why everyone wants to move to California!"

Jennifer smiled again. "How was your flight?"

"It was fine, I guess. It was my first time on a DC-10. You know, your hair looks different in the webcam."

"I'm sure it does. Mom says I need to get bangs in the front."

"No, don't bother—you look fine. This is all still so surreal for me, but I'm glad you're finally convinced that it's not a joke. You mentioned your mother. How is she?"

"She's the same. She's really busy with her work. It's compulsive if you ask me."

"And she's not seeing anyone?"

Jennifer laughed. "*My* mother? She's afraid of relationships. I think she had a bad experience with someone, and that was the end of that. What about your mom? How is she?"

"She's all right. She spends a lot of time with her sister." He thought for a moment and then added, "Wouldn't it be interesting if the two of them met like we have?"

Jennifer shook her head. "I think that might be playing with fire."

Silence.

"I have a question for you," Jennifer said. "Do you pop your ankles in place before putting on your shoes?"

Kevin laughed and said, "Yeah, I do! But it usually depends on how much exercise I did the day before. I think I told you that I like to hike, right? Well, after a good hike, the next day my ankles will just be dying to be popped!"

Jennifer joined in his laughter. "Ha! I knew my theory was right. Some mannerisms are just genetic. My feet do the same thing, but without the hiking part. I'll bet that we have our father's ankles."

"I'll bet you're right about that."

Jennifer took a sip of her tea, and Kevin sipped the water the server had brought him. "I can't imagine how life would have been growing up with a brother," she said. "Most of my friends are stressed out when they talk about their brothers."

"If you were my kid sister, you'd probably be a little stressed out with me too, but I'd still look out after you. The way I see my friends treat their girlfriends—I'd hate for any sister of mine to go through anything like that. I still don't know why some of them go back to those guys."

"It's probably because they don't have good relationships with their own fathers, and their boyfriends fill a void in their emotional lives."

Kevin sat back in his chair, his eyebrows raised. "You sound like you've been studying psychology! But now that I think of it, I agree with you."

"We've got this new teacher who lectures a lot about these things," Jennifer said. "He's kinda cool. I've learned so much this semester about family and relationships. He's the one who inspired me to find out more about our father. By the way, didn't you say you had a surprise for me?"

"I was just about to tell you, Jen. I spoke with him."

"Who?"

"Our father. His name is Leon."

"No way! Are you serious? This is great! How did you ever find him?"

"I tracked his identity code online to a hospital in Colorado. I spoke with a few staff members there and paid one of them to look in their sperm-donor archive database to find his name. Once I had that, I found him on the Internet. He's a deacon in a small church in Colorado now."

"I can't believe it! What did he say? How did he sound?"

"At first he didn't want to talk to me—I think he might have thought I was going to ask him for money—but after I explained that I didn't want anything from him, we had a great conversation. I think he felt a little guilty, but I don't see why he should. I could see some of myself in him. But here's the other thing: We have two other half brothers and sisters, also from sperm donations. One is in Washington, DC, and the other is in Iowa."

"Oh my," Jennifer giggled, "his sperm really got around, didn't it? Can I talk to him?"

"I told him about how we met and everything, and he was touched, but he's happily married with three kids now. So I don't know."

"Do you think he would mind us getting in touch with the family? His three kids are our half brothers and sisters, you know."

"I'm not sure. We didn't talk about that. But I told him I would log in on to his network page once I met you face to face so we could talk to him together. Then we could hook up with Emmanuel and Tracey—those are the kids in DC and Iowa—and have a four-way webcam chat. I have a laptop in my backpack."

"This is so cool! So we'll have a four-way family reunion online. I'd love to go home and tell Mom, but I just don't think she'd take it the right way."

"I know what you mean."

Jennifer twirled her straw in her iced tea and asked, "Do you really have to go back tomorrow night? Can't you stay a little longer?"

"No, my mom thinks I'm hiking this weekend with a friend, and I could only book the hotel for two days, but we could set up our four-way webcam in the hotel lobby tonight."

CHAPTER 10

Principal Franklin leaned back in his big chair, perspiring. He dreaded these types of crises. The school security guard, a local police detective, and Mr. Gunderson looked at him from their chairs on the other side of his desk, but he had no insights. Everything he knew came from the freeze-framed images on his two computer terminals, which showed the last time Theresa Jezebel Jablanski had been seen at school. It had been two and a half weeks since the hallway security camera caught her just as she was leaving Gunderson's classroom before the Easter break.

"There it is—right there," said the security guard, pointing at the screen. "I've had to take that cell phone from her a dozen times. She must have just received a call."

"We've tried to get her cell phone number from her mother," said the detective, "but her mom never even knew she had one. It was probably one of those rechargeable card phones."

"All the kids know about my no-cell-phone policy," said Gunderson. "I never knew she had one on her, and it never rang in my class."

"Keith," Principal Franklin said, "we were looking at the ET data on your kids and found some interesting leads."

"What's ET data?" asked the detective.

"ET means Emotional Intelligence," Franklin said. "We've implemented a new program that helps us collect data on these kids so we can look at their emotional stability at school. I was just about to tell Mr. Gunderson that the data from his kids shows a huge change for two of his students, and one of them is Theresa. Over the last four months she's had more prolonged periods of depression and anger, and we know that her mother has been concerned about a change in her behavior."

"You said there was a change for two students," said the security guard. "Who was the other one?"

"That would be Jennifer. She started out very depressed but has been less depressed these last three months. Most of these kids are on medication, but Jennifer's counselor reports no change in her medication, so I'm not sure what's caused her improvement."

"D'ya think this Jennifer could have anything to do with Theresa's disappearance?" asked the detective.

"I don't think so," said Gunderson. "They're polar opposites. They don't even hang around with the same crowd. But I know why Jennifer's been more positive lately. She let me in on a secret after class one day: she's finally found her father."

"That's right!" said Principal Franklin. "She's the girl who used to cut herself whose father was a sperm donor."

"That's the one! She told me that she found a half-brother somewhere and that the two of them got together to track down their biological father. Now there's been a complete turnaround in her attitude. She's more sociable, and I think she's shared this story with a few of her closer friends."

"I need to talk with this girl," said the detective.

"I think she stays after school for the book club," said Principal Franklin. "They meet in the library—in fact, I think they're meeting now."

The security guard stood up and moved to the door, saying, "I'll see if I can catch her."

The principal, Gunderson, and the detective remained in the office. "The campus library is nearly two buildings away," Franklin told the detective.

"No time like the present," the detective replied. "If this matter isn't resolved immediately, rumors about Theresa's absence could spread and create confusion, and that would be bad for the school's reputation. How about her grades?"

"Her grades don't really show any kind of improvement," Gunderson replied. "She has a sour attitude that may take time and counseling to improve."

"Did you know that the students refer to her mother as the campus cougar?" Franklin interjected. "Her mother even dated one of the custodians here last month. I wouldn't have believed it if I hadn't seen them leaving together after school. Sorry, that probably falls more into the category of gossip than helpful information."

The detective made a note on his small notepad. "No, everything's helpful," he said. "Maybe the poor child just had to get away from Mom. Does she have any other family around?"

"No, and the mom forbids her from seeing her dad," said Principal Franklin. "We've talked with her about the wisdom of—"

The office door swung open, and the security guard and Jennifer stepped in. Her eyes grew large at noticing the crowd and she became fearful that she was somehow in trouble for making contact with her biological father.

"Sit down, Jennifer," said Principal Franklin. She lowered herself onto the chair nearest the door.

"Hey, Jennifer," said Gunderson in his most reassuring voice. "Listen, you're not in any trouble, so you can take it easy, okay?"

Jennifer blushed and said in a voice just above a whisper, "I was just trying to think about what I must have done wrong."

Principal Franklin leaned back in his chair. "I'm sorry if I scared you," he said. "We just need to ask you some questions about one of your classmates, all right? You'll be able to get back to your book club soon. What book are you going through this month?"

"It's a historical fiction called *Destiny's Spear*," Jennifer replied, her voice a little stronger.

"Do you like it?" the principal asked.

"Yeah. It's really exciting."

"Good. I like historical fiction too." Franklin turned his chair and pointed to the freeze-framed image from the security camera. "Now, Jennifer, do you see that computer screen?"

"Yes, that's the hallway where Mr. Gunderson's class is."

"That's right. Take a closer look. Who do you see in that picture?"

Jennifer hesitated. "I don't know," she said at last. "I can't really make out their faces. Oh! I think that's Theresa. She's the only one I know with a purse like that. Has she come back?"

"What do you mean?" Franklin asked, his voice even.

"She's been away since Easter break, and I thought she must have come back."

"Do you know where she went?" asked the detective.

"She said she was going to meet someone in Florida. I assumed that everyone knew about it."

The detective and the principal exchanged glances. "Did she say who she was going to see there?" the principal asked.

"Some guy she met on the Internet. She said she contacted this young guy who runs a hotel, and he arranged for her to get a job interview." She looked one by one at the other four faces in the room, all of which had turned grim.

"But it's still the middle of the school year," said Gunderson gently. "Did she plan to stay and work there?"

"I don't think she planned to stay very long," Jennifer said. "She was just going to have fun and hang around a week during spring break and see if she could go back there for a summer job."

"Do you know the name of the hotel?"

"No. Doesn't her mother know?"

Principal Franklin leaned forward, resting his forearms on his desk. "Jennifer," he said, "no one knows where she is, and we think she might be in trouble."

"But she couldn't be!" said Jennifer. "She said she really got to know this guy and—"

The detective interrupted. "Has she been chatting with this guy online for a long time?"

"I don't know. She just told me that she met him."

"But why did she tell you all these things?" asked Gunderson. "Was anyone else there when she told you?"

"No." Jennifer then took a moment to think about the conversation she had had with Theresa before spring break. They were at Jennifer's locker, and she was showing her friends a picture of her half-brother, Kevin.

"I remember that I was just finished talking with another friend about a family conference call with my half-brother. Then Theresa told me that she had met a nice guy online and that they were finally going to meet."

"So, when she heard you talking about your half-brother, she stepped in to talk about this guy?" Gunderson asked.

"That's right, sir. She's always been like that. It's like whenever you talk about something cool, she has to jump in and share something about herself too. But most times her stories aren't even true."

"So it's possible that she was lying about the whole story with this Florida guy?" Franklin asked.

"It's possible, Mr. Franklin," she said, "but she seemed really sincere when she spoke about him. I think she was telling the truth this time. Gosh, I hope she's all right."

CHAPTER 11

Her job was simple: clean the filthy toilets in the main lobby with abrasive powder; keep the salad bar looking fresh for new residents, even if it meant recycling uneaten parsley, lemon wedges, and sliced tomatoes from the plates of previous customers, as these items could continue to appear fresh for as much as four days; and help round up young girls like herself to coax them into working at the hotel for minimum wage. Her salary was fair, she had her own studio at the hotel, and she was off all day on Wednesdays with pay. Although it had been an exciting spring break adventure at first, giving her exposure to college students and world travelers, by now it was something different. She had been spoiled at first but then she was drugged with Rohypnol to lower her inhibitions, and seduced. She had intended to return home to California after spring break, but she began to feel more at home with Keiko, the charming, half-Cuban proprietor she met online. She felt protected and cared for by him.

Keiko suggested that she extend her stay and miss the last semester of school, arguing that she could always make up the classwork in summer school, so she stayed. She never knew that she was becoming just another cog in the wheel of an underground slave trade network for teenage runaways.

At 6:30 a.m. one morning, Keiko stood outside her studio door wearing a bleached-white, light cotton, button-down shirt with the top three buttons left open. He was known for his wardrobe of Latin shirts that showed his muscular chest.

"Theresa! Theresa!" he called as he knocked at her door.

Theresa appeared. "Hi," she said, yawning. "I'm up. Had a kind of hard night last night. I finally decided to write my mom to let her know that I'll be staying until summer."

"You wrote her?" Keiko said, striding into the tiny room. "Who writes anymore? You could have called."

Theresa laughed. "Not my mom. She's on the phone so much I would have had to leave a message in her voice mail anyway. Then it would have taken her three days to finally listen to it."

"Will she agree with your staying?"

"Yeah. I turn eighteen in two weeks anyway, so it doesn't matter if she agrees or not."

"Well, listen: there are five new girls who went to the homeless shelter last night. I don't know how long they'll stay, but you need to talk to them before the church people get there this afternoon."

"I thought they only came on Sundays."

"No, they used to come on Sundays. Now they're coming all week."

"What do they do with these people?"

"You know, they give them donations and Bibles and that kind of thing, but they're not giving out any jobs like we are. That's why most of our ladies come from there."

The homeless shelter had been constructed in the center of town deliberately. People from the neighboring communities called it "God's Hood" because it stood out as an oasis of love and charity in a blighted community of corruption, prostitution, and drug dealing. It was different from other shelters, and people felt safe there. Since it was their policy never to turn away anyone who had a need, sometimes they had to place roadblocks on their street at night to make room for small tents, beds, and a portable soup kitchen outdoors after they reached maximum capacity indoors. Volunteer teachers, dentists, and doctors visited around the clock to provide services and check up on their burgeoning residents. During simpler times, the shelter was frequented primarily by white men in need of employment, so it allowed local businesses to visit and recruit for entry-level jobs. Now however, demographics were changing. Runaway teen mothers and high school dropouts of every race had become the majority of their clientele, and a high percentage were addicts, making it nearly impossible to communicate rationally. The staff of volunteers saw these young women and girls as "unreachable and unteachable," but a local community church's outreach team saw them differently.

The shelter had a grand outdoor patio where itinerant residents could enjoy a clean environment while they ate breakfast and lunch. There was something about this area that helped restore the residents' dignity. A "business bench" sat in a far corner for local store owners who wanted to conduct simple interviews for custodians, maids, and secretaries, but it was used more and more by local outreach volunteers from the community Christian fellowship group. It was an ideal place for meeting new residents, even preaching.

Theresa tapped on the security gate and a uniformed guard appeared. "Hi," Theresa said, "I'm recruiting for the Fedala Sands Hotel. Is this a good time to visit?" Theresa reached into her purse and presented a business card.

"Oh," the guard said, "you must work with Keiko."

"Yes," she responded, smiling, "he's my boss."

"Okay, step inside. Someone from a local church is still using the business bench, but he should be finished soon."

Theresa walked across the tile patio floor, sliding her high heels forward with each measured step like a roller skater, trying not to attract any attention.

"It's as real today as it was two thousand years ago." The young preacher's voice echoed off the patio walls. "Jesus still saves. God still loves you and has a plan for your life."

The echo, so loud that it could be heard from across the street, startled Theresa.

"Won't you receive him in your heart by faith?" the preacher continued, his voice rising. "Some of you have tried everything to fill the voids in your hearts, and you've come to the end of your resources. You've left your families. You've tried drugs, illicit sex, and other shameful things, trying to satisfy the longing in your hearts. But only Jesus can satisfy completely. Only he can take that place. Only he can resurrect your dead life and produce a new one."

The words caught her off guard, and she stopped to listen. Something the preacher said about leaving one's family and having an empty heart struck her, and as the preacher went on, she became certain that someone had told him about her life. How else could he have known about the drug abuse and the disdain she had for her own mother?

His voice echoed in her brain. "What I am saying is this: Despite your past, God still loves you. The Bible says that while we were yet sinners, Christ died for us. This means that you don't have to try to clean yourself up before coming to him. You couldn't clean yourself up enough. Just surrender to him. Ask him to forgive you of your sins and commit your life to following him."

Theresa sensed something real in what the preacher was saying, but it created an internal conflict within her. She didn't move. People began to walk toward the preacher's makeshift platform. His words were reassuring, she thought, but what he was asking sounded too easy. Something within her wanted to approach the business bench with the others who were gathering to pray, but she fought against it. She looked at the women and thought that at least she was not as desperate as they appeared; many had visible bruises, and others were so wild-eyed that she was certain they were suffering from mental illnesses. At least she had Keiko.

"Excuse me, honey," said a middle-aged women as she placed her hand on Theresa's shoulder, "but are you a part of this man's ministry?"

"Me? Oh, no. I'm just waiting for him to finish. I'm recruiting girls for work at a local hotel nearby."

"You are? Which hotel?"

"The Fedala Sands Hotel."

"The Fedala Sands?" she said, raising a penciled eyebrow. "Isn't that the one a few blocks from the train station?"

"That's the one," said Theresa.

Instantly the woman's continence changed from friendly to repulsed. Her face even appeared to grow older as she frowned at Theresa and looked her up and down in obvious suspicion.

"Is there something wrong?" asked Theresa.

"Yes, child, a lot of things are wrong! Don't you know what kinda place that is?"

"It's just a hotel." Then she added, muttering, "though I know it's not the cleanest one around."

"No, sweetie, it's not the place that's unclean; it's the people."

"What are you talking about?"

"Child, we have two girls in this shelter here who escaped from that place. It's a prostitution ring, and they look for runaway girls. They drug them up until they're out of their minds, and then they trade 'em like slaves."

"I don't believe that! I've been there nearly a month, and I haven't seen any of that."

"Of course not," said the woman, shaking her head. "They're sneaky. They do a good job covering it up, and the big boss—they call him Reeko or something—"

"You mean Keiko?"

"Yes, that's him: Keiko. He has connections with the local police and the city council. That's why they turn their heads and don't investigate him."

"Listen," Theresa said, rising up in Keiko's defense, "all the girls I know choose to stay there for work. All of them are eighteen or older, and nobody is forcing them to do anything."

"Honey, they drug them up! They put the drugs in their food so they can't figure anything out anymore." Then she added reflectively, "Most of them never had much sense anyway. You better get out of there."

"So you're telling me that these girls don't get outta there because they're drugged? That can't be. I talk to them every day."

"Honey, they become addicts! Do you know what an addict is? It might be that some stay there because they have no place else to go, but most of them get addicted to these drugs, and they stay there for a fix. They'll do anything for another hit!"

"Thank you for sharing your thoughts with me," Theresa said, turning away, but I don't think you've got your story right." Just then the young pastor approached, holding reading materials and small hand-outs.

"Hello, ladies," he said with a smile.

"Good morning," Theresa and the woman said in unison, their faces tight.

"I'm Pastor Bill."

"Hi, pastor, I'm Dorothea," said the other woman.

"And I'm Theresa. I was just waiting to set things up at the bench over there."

"Are you handing out flyers?" Pastor Bill asked.

"I'm helping to recruit girls for part-time work at one of the local hotels," she said with a feigned smile. Dorothea's face flushed, and she balled one hand into a fist.

"I'm sure that most of these ladies will jump at the chance to do anything they might qualify for," said the pastor. "Can I give you something to read?" he added, extending one of his flyers to her.

Theresa reached out to take the flyer, formatted in simple comic book fashion. She folded it in half and placed it in her purse.

"Thanks," she said, "but I'd better start setting things up before people start leaving." Theresa nodded at the pastor and Dorothea before taking her cards and flyers to the community table. She fanned out several colorful flyers and placed a few hotel business cards just next to them. Several women were already waiting at the table for information.

"Can I look at this?" inquired a small voice from behind her.

Theresa turned around and looked into the pretty face of a young girl with caramel-colored skin. She was unusually tall, had thick, wavy hair, and appeared to have a permanent smile, though the state of her teeth bore testimony to an unbalanced diet and poor dental hygiene. She was wearing mismatched clothes that Theresa deduced must have come from donations at the shelter.

"I'm Theresa. I work at one of the local hotels here."

"I'm Miya," the girl replied in accented English. "Can I see this one?" She pointed at one of the flyers on the table.

"Sure, here you go," said Theresa, handing her the item. "You speak English well."

"Just so-so. I learn English now. You give work to women?"

"Yes, I do."

"What kind?"

"It depends. Some girls cook in the restaurant. Some girls clean the rooms. Some girls

dance in the shows—"

Miya's eyes lit up. "Dance in the shows?" she said. "I dance in my country! It's a kind of—how do you say—cultural dancing. Do you know cultural dancing?"

"No, not really. But, you know, you look like a dancer."

"Thank you."

"I'm sure my boss would be interested in meeting you."

"Your boss?"

"Yeah, at the hotel. I could take you there this afternoon to talk with him. What time do you have to be back here?"

"They tell us they lock the doors at seven o'clock at night."

"Give me about ten minutes to see if anyone else wants to come. I know there are five new girls who came to stay here for a while. Will they let you leave the shelter for the afternoon?"

"Oh, yes, but we must give our names to the office man inside. They tell us they want us to leave in the afternoon to look for jobs."

"Good. Why don't you go tell them now that you'll be leaving this afternoon with me? By the time you get back, we can go."

"You will wait for me?"

"Yes, I'll wait here."

Miya walked toward the office at a rapid pace. Theresa could see that she was overjoyed about the possibility of working at the hotel and thought she would make a great dancer: she had the physique and wouldn't have to speak much. Soon Miya returned wearing a light pink sweater and carrying a simple sack lunch and enough bus tokens to get across town and back.

"I'm ready," she said as she returned to the patio.

"It looks like it'll be just us this time," Theresa said. "No one else is coming."

"Oh good!" Miya giggled, "Now they have to choose me."

Theresa and Miya gathered up the hotel literature and walked to the security gate. The guard smiled and nodded at Miya before unlocking the steel door. "Be sure to be back before seven," he said.

When they stepped outside, they were taken back by the stench of human urine and the evidence of poverty just outside the gate. Accelerating their steps, they could not help but notice the dark, broken bottles strewn across the streets, filthy wrappers, and bags from fast-food restaurants that rolled like tumbleweeds against the curbs, and the zombielike, malnourished passersby.

"I guess it's easy to forget where you are when you stay at the shelter," said Theresa. "It's sad."

"Yes, we have places like this in my country, too."

"Why did you leave your country?"

Miya hesitated. "They asked me many personal questions at the shelter, but you are the first to ask why I left," she said.

"It's okay if you don't want to talk about it," said Theresa. "I left my home too. My mother was driving me crazy."

Miya stopped walking and stared at Theresa. "You left because of your mother? Does she know you are here?"

"No, not yet. I had to write her."

"Won't she be worried about you?"

"Not really," she said.

"But what about your father? He will come looking for you, won't he?"

"No, I haven't talked to him in a long time."

"I'm sorry to be hearing that. Both my parents sent me to leave my country for protection. There were some bad men saying to my father that they will do bad things to us if he didn't help them. They were criminals in our government."

"So why are you at the homeless shelter?" asked Theresa.

"I was supposed to live with a family friend and apply for asylum here. He was my father's friend from years ago. But when I got there, his wife didn't want me there."

"Miya, how long have you been in this country?"

"I think maybe eight days."

"There are a lot of things you need to learn about our culture here."

Though crowded, the bus ride across town became more enjoyable as the route led them away from the inner city and onto greener streets. The sight of trees and public buildings untouched by gang-related graffiti reassured Miya's faith that all humanity was not lost. She gestured toward the flyer that poked out of Theresa's purse.

"Isn't that clever?" she said, pointing to the flyer. "In my country, churches don't make things

like that."

"You mean this propaganda?" Theresa unfolded the literature. "I can't believe they waste paper on this."

"Oh, you don't agree with it?"

"No I don't. I don't have time for God, which is okay because I know He doesn't have time for me either. Ever since I was born, no one has had time for me."

"I think you should try to know Him more," said Miya gently. "I think you don't understand what He did for you already."

"You sound like one of my high school teachers," said Theresa.

The bus's air breaks made a hushing sound, and they came to a stop. It was the end of the line, and everyone stood up. "This is our stop," said Theresa. "We've only two blocks to walk to the hotel. Come on."

They descended from the bus, taking deep breaths. Though the warm air was mingled with smog, it was more pleasant than the air of the stuffy bus or the putrid odors of the inner city.

Miya walked briskly, her long legs carrying her forward at almost twice Theresa's pace. They passed small family shops before seeing the hotel from a distance and a man standing at the entrance.

"Hey, look," said Theresa. "That's my boss. That's Keiko."

Theresa waved as they slowed their pace to avoid the small puddles in the aging sidewalk that was still drenched from an afternoon rinse with a water hose. Theresa smiled and stood on her tiptoe to kiss Keiko on the cheek. He put an arm around her, but his eyes were fixed on Miya.

"I'm glad I caught you," he said. "I was just about to leave."

"Where are you going?" Theresa asked. I want to introduce you to a new applicant. She can't stay too long."

"It's okay," Keiko said turning to Miya. "I was just going to see someone at City Hall, but he can wait. And what is your name, my dear?"

"My name is Miya, sir."

"Miya?" he said. "The name is as beautiful as you are."

"Thank you," Miya replied, lowering her eyes.

"Tell me, Miya, do you have any experience in hotel work?"

"Hotel work? No, but in my country I do cultural dancing. Miss Theresa said I could maybe do the cultural dances for you here."

A slithery grin crossed Keiko's face. "Why, yes! You look every bit like a dancer should look," he said. "Good work, Theresa! Let's go to my office to talk, eh?"

Keiko placed his arm around Theresa's shoulder and guided her into the foyer while Miya followed behind. They passed two women carrying mops and buckets, and both smiled at Keiko but glared at Miya. Keiko leaned toward Theresa and whispered, "She's perfect. Why don't you go get yourself something to eat? I need to talk with Miya privately."

Something told Theresa not to leave Miya alone. "How long will it take?" she asked. "I have to get her back to the shelter before it gets dark, and I wanted to show her around a little."

"It won't take long at all. We're just going to get acquainted."

They were standing in front of the hotel kitchen, and she could smell the greasy odor from the deep fryers emanating through the double doors.

"Hey, Frank!" yelled Keiko toward the doors. "Bring a couple of plates to my office, eh? One for me and one for the lady." He pointed to Miya and winked.

"Two hot ones coming up," came Frank's reply.

"Theresa, you can hang out in the kitchen for a bit if you want," Keiko said. "Miya and I will be in my office for about half an hour, okay?"

"Okay, Keiko," Theresa said, beginning to tremble. "I'll wait for her in the kitchen."

Keiko smiled at Miya and gestured that she should walk next to him. Miya turned and waved at Theresa, who said, "I'll come get ya in thirty minutes."

Keiko's and Miya's footsteps echoed on the polished oak floors until they reached his office door. Then Keiko inserted his key, opened the door, and ushered Miya inside. Before stepping in behind her, he glanced back at Theresa, who was still watching them from down the hallway. His countenance had changed; she had never seen that expression before. He gave her a forced, toothy smile and closed the door behind him.

Theresa heard a loud knocking at the kitchen window behind her. "Hey, Theresa," said Frank, "you wanna bite before we close da kitchen?"

"Yes, thanks," Theresa said, her eyes still on the spot where Keiko had stood a moment before. "I'll just eat it here in the foyer if that's okay." She hated the hotel food; they didn't change the frying oil often enough, and she had once seen cockroaches the size of mice near the second fryer.

"On second thought, could you just make me a salad?" she said through the glass. Frank gave her a thumbs-up.

Theresa stood near the window so she could watch Frank. He prepared two plates of fried chicken patties and French fries, which she assumed were for Miya and Keiko. Then he poured a glass of iced tea and, before pouring the second one, slipped his hand into his pocket and pulled out a small glass vial filled with white powder. He shook it, opened it, and poured the powder into the second glass, tapping the packet gently against the rim before filling the glass with tea. Theresa turned away from the window, her mind racing back to the argument she had with Dorothea at the shelter. "Could it be true?" she thought, "Could they be drugging these girls to traffic them?"

"Hey, Theresa!" Frank's voice sounded from behind her. Startled, she jumped and almost knocked the two trays of food from his hands.

"Whoa, careful there, honey," he said. "Just let me give Keiko and the new girl their food and I'll be right back with that salad, all right?"

Theresa nodded. She watched him walk down the hall, knock on Keiko's door, and step inside with the trays.

"Maybe it was only powdered drink mix," she thought. "They put powdered drink mix in all the drinks here for extra flavor. Then why did he take it from his pocket? Something is wrong."

The office door opened and closed, and Frank walked toward her, smiling. "Let me get you that salad now—give me a minute," he said.

Theresa had completely lost her appetite, and after three minutes that loss of appetite turned to panic. She was sick with worry for Miya.

Suddenly, the door to Keiko's office flew open, and Keiko ran out, yelling, "Frank! Get me glass of milk!" He ran down the hall and into the kitchen, oblivious to Theresa. She ran to Keiko's office, where she saw Miya staggering in an attempt to rise from the floor. Her face was bright red and drenched with perspiration, and she looked as if she were about to vomit.

"I fell down," she moaned, tears welling in her eyes, "I don't feel good."

"Miya, listen to me," said Theresa, pulling her to her feet. "We gotta get out of here, and we're going right through that window."

She dragged Miya around Keiko's desk, where the half-eaten plates of food and empty glasses sat. She threw the window open pushed Miya through it to the grass outside.

"Hey! Stop! What do you think you're doing?" yelled Keiko, dropping the full glass of milk he was carrying. Theresa said nothing as she finished lowering Miya down from the window. Then she hopped out, landing next to her in the grass. Hand-in-hand, they ran away.

Frank ran in from the kitchen. "What's up? Where's the girl?"

"Theresa took off with her," Keiko said. "They went out the window!"

"You think she knows something?"

"She must. Come on. They're probably going to the bus station."

Keiko opened his desk drawer, pulled out his handgun, and slid it in his inside coat pocket.

CHAPTER 12

Jennifer and Kevin had each told their mothers they would be spending the weekend at a friend's house, but they planned to meet at the Rocky Mountain Metropolitan airport in Colorado at 6:30 p.m. to finally meeting their biological father and his family after several weeks of exchanging emails. The evening mountain air carried a brisk chill.

"Let me carry that for you," Kevin said, taking hold of the handle of Jennifer's bag.

"It's good to know my brother is a gentleman," she said, smiling. "I was hoping you'd ask."

"So far you're the only real sister I've met, so that makes you special. I'm just glad you're not one of those persnickety gals who tries to prove she can lift her own bags without a man's help."

"Yeah, I used to think like that, but I feel I'm finally growing up. What's your room number at the hotel?"

"I'm in 427, and I booked 429 for you."

"Did you actually book a room for me? I already made a reservation for myself."

"I didn't want to risk being separated. It would have been awkward with me on the fourth floor and you all the way on the twelfth or something. Sometimes conventions come through town and fill up the hotels. Then, before you know it, all they have left is a studio somewhere on the ground floor next to the ice machines. But don't worry," he added. "They'll give you a refund."

Jennifer was pleasantly surprised by her brother's display of care for her well-being. Although they had not yet been acquainted for six months, she felt a strong sense of family when she was near him.

The taxi ride to the hotel was something of a sightseeing tour for them, as it seemed that the driver made every attempt to pass by trendy cafes, picturesque mountain trails, local hiking centers, and small lakes for boating.

"You two plan to stay long?" the driver asked, looking back at them in the rearview mirror.

"Not really. Just for the weekend," replied Kevin.

"What brings you through these parts?" the driver asked as the cab passed a row of trendy cafes.

"We're here for a family reunion," said Jennifer, "It feels like a paradise here. The mountains are breathtaking!"

"Yeah, a lot of tourists want to come back here to retire because of our mountains."

"I can see why," said Kevin. "It seems very restful."

"It used to be a lot more restful until crazy kids started shooting up schools and public theaters. My cousin's niece was injured in one of those shootings. I just can't understand what gets into a young person's mind to create that type of sickness."

Jennifer was quiet a moment before she said, "I understand exactly where you're coming from, but we have to understand how these kids are raised and the things they're exposed to while growing up."

"The thing that gets me," the driver said, slowing for a stoplight, "is that a lot of these kids come from such rich families. I mean, they have almost anything they want."

"Right," said Kevin. "They can have almost anything they want, but they probably never had what they needed.

The silence in the taxi was like the type of silence that follows a prayer request. No one knew what to say.

Two hundred feet ahead of them, the lights on the hotel grew brighter as the vehicle made its way up the ramp to park at the main entrance.

When Kevin opened his wallet to pay for the cab, the driver said, "I tell ya what, son: it's on the house."

"Oh, no," said Kevin, "you're entitled to your pay."

"Well, now, I know I'm entitled to it, but I like what you said. It made a lot of sense, and I won't forget it."

Kevin smiled and extended his hand. The two shook hands, nodded, and waved goodbye.

The hotel lobby was a thoroughfare of travelers. Dozens of youth groups wore matching variations of tie-dyed shirts and colored hats, checking in for a hiking convention that was taking place during the extended weekend. "I told you there might be a convention," said Kevin. "Look at this crowd!"

"I know. This is too much. You know, I just want to call Dad so he can pick us up," said Jennifer. "Once we get our keys, we can call him to come get us and then rest at his place. What do you think? Do you mind?"

"I say it sounds like a plan," said Kevin, "but let's not wait too long because I know they're planning a dinner."

Kevin walked to a corner of the lobby and took out his cell phone. He had preregistered his father's cell number so he could call once he arrived at the airport. He punched the keys to a local number and pressed the small receiver against his face.

"Hello? a muffled voice said.

"Hello. May I speak with Leon, please?"

"This is Leon. Is that you, Kevin?"

"Yeah, it's me! And I've got Jenny here with me at the hotel."

"Great! Hey, I'm sorry, but I can barely hear you. We're outside trying to start a barbecue. Are you all checked in yet?"

"Not yet. We just got here, and there are a lot of people in line to register."

"Must be for the camping trips. It happens every year at this time. Listen, I'm going to give you some time to check in and catch your breath. I'll be able to come and get you in about half an hour. The barbecue will be up and running by then. How's that sound?"

"That'll work. Thank you! I'll call you back in an hour."

"Fine. I'll talk with you soon!"

While Kevin called their father, Jennifer sat down on her luggage to rest, and her eyes turned to a large television screen that hung on the center wall of the hotel lobby. A cable news channel was broadcasting a story about a tragic accident at an amusement park in Florida, and Jennifer felt herself being drawn into the drama. She stood up and walked closer to the television screen to read the stream of information than ran under the picture: "Mangled body of unidentified young woman found under rollercoaster."

She stepped closer to listen.

"It's a pity, isn't it?" said a woman from behind her.

Jennifer turned around, surprised. "Do you know what happened?" she asked.

"They've been running that story all morning. The city council somewhere in Florida just approved the opening of a new amusement park—one of the council members is a part owner. They found a young woman's body in one of the tunnel rides so beat up that she's beyond recognition. The strange thing is that she couldn't have fallen off the ride because you can't even get on if you don't have at least one person with you. And no one remembers seeing anyone dressed like she was."

"Didn't she have any identification?"

"No, apparently not. She had some drugs in her system, though."

Before Jennifer could ask another question, Kevin appeared from behind her and said, "He'll be here in about five minutes."

"But we haven't even checked in yet," said Jennifer. She wanted to stay to follow the story.

"I know. I spoke to the concierge. He said their computers are down and it may take a while, so they're keeping our bags behind the front desk counter until we get back. It's better if we just go now."

"All right. I'm going to go to the restroom for a minute."

"Sure, I'll be waiting in that area over there by the door."

Kevin found the only comfortable place of solace left in the lobby next to the main doors and settled into a loveseat. He picked up a magazine and opened it to an ad about a new hybrid truck, a dazzling sky-blue beast with turbine cyclone mag wheels.

"That may look good in a magazine but it'll never make it up some of our mountains," came a man's voice from behind him.

Leon walked around to face Kevin, who immediately recognized his biological father, though he looked younger in person than he had on the webcam. He lost his breath for a moment, and his legs felt heavy, but he managed to stand up and face him. They were nearly the same height. Kevin extended his hand, to which Leon responded by grasping it and pulling him close to hug him.

"How are you, Kevin?" Leon said, his voice shaking. "I can't believe it! I feel like I'm looking at my high school senior photo when I see you. You look good, son. I'm sorry—can I call you son?"

"Sure you can."

"I'll tell you, when you and Jennifer contacted me, I never knew how much joy it would give me to meet you—my own flesh and blood."

"Thanks, Jennifer and I both feel as if we're coming to an end of a journey. We have so many things we want to ask you."

"I know, I know. And I have many things to share with both of you."

Jennifer was watching from a distance, intimidated at the site of her father. "How should I greet him?" she thought. But before she could answer the question for herself, Kevin spotted her. Noticing Kevin's change in focus, Leon turned around, looked at her, and smiled. Although Jennifer remained motionless, her face became radiant.

Leon strode to her side. "Can I give you a hug, Jennifer?" he asked.

Unable to speak, Jennifer nodded. He put his arms around her, and they embraced. Jennifer's eyes welled up in tears. During the embrace, Leon noticed the faint scars on her arms and felt a pang of guilt for not having been in her life. He stood back to look at the two together.

"You are wonderful people," he said, choking up. "You've gone to such great lengths to meet me. Let's sit down for a moment." They arranged themselves around the loveseat in the waiting area.

"Do you mind if we call you Dad?" asked Jennifer.

"No, sweetie, I'd be honored," Leon said as he sat down. "Gosh, what a sight! You can't imagine how I feel just looking at the two of you, but I wanted to talk with you a little before taking you back home. First, I need to say I'm sorry. You are my children, yet you never knew me."

"That's okay, Dad," said Kevin. "You don't have to apologize."

"Thank you for saying that, but I really do need to apologize. I was a completely different person when I donated ... to that clinic. It was a type of cultural thing this country was going through when women thought they could remain independent in raising children by themselves. But now we're all seeing the long-term effects this has on kids and our whole society. My generation was pretty ignorant about these things. Children are meant to have a father and a mother; if we had just listened more to what nature and history teaches us, we'd all be better off now. A few moments ago when we met, Kevin, you said that you two felt as if you were coming to the end of a journey. Well, I want you to see this now as the beginning of a new journey—but not just with me. I'm going to take you to my home, where you're going to meet your other half brothers and sisters. We're having a barbecue to celebrate, and we'll all get acquainted."

"That sounds great," Kevin said. Jennifer nodded and bit her lip.

"But then what?" Leon continued. "Over the last several weeks I've told you about how I became a deacon in my church. I've tried to tell you, without putting any pressure on you, how God has changed my life, and I've been praying for you. In fact, the whole family has been praying and fasting for you two to encounter God the way we have. You see, I'm afraid that I can never make up for my absence in your past, but you have a heavenly Father who has been watching you all this time, and He wants you to continue your journey with Him because He has a plan and purpose for you. It was a good thing that you sought me out, as it's our dads who give us a sense of identity and security, but you have a heavenly Father who can take you beyond that. All you need to do is come to Him by putting your faith in His son!"

Kevin and Jennifer were spellbound. They had chatted with each other online about their dad's work in the church and how his faith seemed so simple yet genuine. Though they had suspected that he might try to convert them, they trusted him. At first, they felt awkward talking to each other about it, but now they felt differently. Their dad's words were sensible, and because they trusted him, they were able to agree with him and put their faith in Jesus Christ. The three of them held hands, and Leon led them in prayer. They prayed for the forgiveness of their sins, they prayed for the needs of their mothers, and they prayed for their mothers' eternal salvation.

Onlookers in the lobby stopped and watched, touched by the hallowed sight of their shared prayer.

When the prayer was finished, Leon said, "I want you two to stay the night at our place. Never mind about checking in here at the hotel. We've got two rooms already set up, so let's get your bags and get to that barbecue!"

CHAPTER 13

The bag had been tagged with the number 226, a pale-yellow tag that hung down as lifeless as the cold contents it represented. It was not a luggage bag but a body bag, and the lonely, unidentified corpse inside had been at the county morgue for more than two weeks. Despite the evidence of physical struggle, the cause of death was determined to be multiple injuries resulting from an accident on an amusement park ride. No one called about her, no one came to identify her, and the local sheriff reluctantly gave the final okay to have her buried in an unmarked grave—just another teenaged runaway. Out of respect, they lowered her pale body into the earth along with a remnant of religious writing that had been found in her pocket. It was a torn piece of a flyer, illustrated in comic-book fashion, about eternal life.

The staff at the homeless shelter were sad to lose her but pleased to see Miya reunite with her family when both of her parents, along with her brothers and sisters, were granted political asylum, and her father obtained a professorship at a local university. They would be able to become citizens within five years.

"Miya, be sure to come back to visit once in a while, okay?" said the director when Miya was saying her final farewells.

"Thank you," Miya replied. "I think I can come back sometimes with the church outreach. Pastor Bill told to my father that he comes at least one time a month and that I can come with him."

"Then we'll definitely look forward to seeing you. It looks like he'll want to use you to help set up the outreach at the business bench."

"Maybe, but I also want to talk with the other women."

"Good, good!" Then the director's face grew serious. "Miya," he asked, "what happened to that woman from the hotel who took you for an interview some time ago? We haven't seen her for a while."

"I haven't seen her since that day when we had to leave the hotel. I was feeling sick, and she rushed me out of her boss's office. I think I ate something bad. I thought she would take me to the hospital, but when we ran for the bus and I got on, her boss drove up in a car, and she ran in another direction and didn't get on the bus. So I just came back here."

Made in the USA
Middletown, DE
09 December 2021

54855886R00068